The Pool of Pink Lilies

by

JOYCE DINGWELL

Harlequin Books

TORONTO • LONDON • LOS ANGELES • AMSTERDAM
SYDNEY • HAMBURG • PARIS • STOCKHOLM • ATHENS • TOKYO

Original hardcover edition published in 1970
by Mills & Boon Limited

ISBN 0-373-01688-3

Harlequin edition published May 1973

Second printing September 1980

Printed in Canada

CHAPTER ONE

BOMBAY from the Tourist Class gangplank of the *Fairadventure*. Bombay at last. Little enough to see as from most docks serving big cities, but at this pallid, unarranged, pre-dawn hour, for bad weather following Colombo had put the *Fairadventure* back eighteen hours, with no small brown boys cartwheeling entertainingly for pennies, no Indian women meeting the ship and looking like bright butterflies in their gay saris, even worse than drab. In Greer's and Holly's case a distinct let-down after two weeks of sea and thrice that of anticipation. Particularly, Greer thought wretchedly, a let-down for her younger sister Holly.

Stepsister, really, but as beloved as any blood sister could ever have been – dear, frail, badly-named Holly, as contrasted to glossy green and glowing scarlet as she could be. What, wondered Greer, is Holly thinking now?

For almost two months, ever since Uncle Randall's Sydney visit, Holly had talked of nothing else but Bombay, of Uncle Randall's residence some distance out of the city, of the moment when they arrived at the wharf, of all the pulsing glitter, the intoxicating excitement, the clamour and glamour of what was generally agreed was the ideal first experience of India.

Holly had read Bombay, breathed it, dreamed it, lived it. She knew the names of its streets, its parks, its bazaars. She knew its population, its climate, its exports, it activities. Staying at home all day she had embraced it as Greer, at work, had never done. Not, thought Greer, that she herself would have embraced it even had she had the time. Not when the idea sprung as it had from Uncle Randall.

Yet here she was visiting Uncle Randall, even more

than that accepting a 'kind of post' to Uncle and his new wife Arlene – 'A luxury passage,' Uncle Randall had dangled, 'pennies for side trips and boat fun, then later at Bombay the best of board for you both, with more pennies to spend, and, believe me' ... a shrewd eye on the susceptible Holly ... 'there's pretty things a-plenty to spend your money on in Bombay.'

'Money for doing what?' Greer had asked pointblank of that 'kind of post' Uncle Randall had hinted at.

'Mostly just being there,' Uncle Randall had said smoothly, 'company for Arlene.'

It had sounded unsatisfactory, and Greer would have refused instantly but for the brightness in Holly's tired blue eyes. All at once they had been shining cornflowers. Two fingers of carnation pink had touched her pale cheeks.

'India!' Holly had breathed.

'You like the sound of it, don't you?' Uncle Randall had smiled, noting with obvious approval how pretty Holly became when she was animated. 'You'll like the real thing better, m'dear.'

'It's out of the question, of course,' Greer had endeavoured to insert.

Uncle Randall had ignored Greer and concentrated on Holly. 'Best berths,' he had repeated. 'Every possible extra. Buy what you like from the signed cheque I'll leave with the Purser. Lovely things in the ship's shop. Fabulous stuff in Colombo.'

'Holly has been ill,' Greer had tried again. 'The climate in Bombay—'

'Is not as bad as it's made out to be. In fact the bad reputation only ever came from the Indians ... the Europeans quite like it, no great extremes, and the only rains during the monsoon.'

'This virus that Holly picked up—' It had been a disturbing, baffling infection, and because Holly was frail before the onset even more difficult than usual to eradicate. 'This—'

6

'She looks all right to me,' Uncle Randall had intervened flatteringly. 'Looks a peach.'

The trouble, Greer thought now as she had thought then, had been that Holly did not *know* him, had never set eyes on him before he had turned up at the flat that day, turned up when Greer was at work. When Greer had arrived home he had had Holly enchanted with his compliments and praise. He had had her won with his Indian talk.

Afterwards it had seemed pointless to say to the girl, 'Darling, he's new to you, but not to me. He's my uncle, not yours. Every encounter with Uncle Randall has been a catastrophe. When you were in hospital that awful time that Stephen' ... Stephen had been Holly's father and Greer's stepfather, yet equally loved ... 'died, and Uncle Randall "kindly" took Mother and me in, it was horrible, it was a nightmare. I really believe it started Mother's end.' Yes, pointless ... and cruel? ... to shining cornflower eyes and soft carnation cheeks. Pointless to try to relate many mean acts. For instance that hard winter following Stephen's death, Holly fortunately still away, when Uncle's 'hospitality' to his sister and niece had really meant his disastrous dwindling of their already restricted funds. Pointless and cruel, Greer knew, to sweetly parted lips that shaped only one word: Bombay.

'Why must it be Bombay?' Greer had begged at last.

'Because – well, because it's *there*, isn't it? I mean it's the only place that has ever become even remotely possible. Oh, Greer, Greer, agree, please agree.'

'We'll see what Doctor Jenner has to say, then,' Greer had answered, and had been saddened at Holly's crumpled little face.

'He'll never say yes,' Holly had sighed.

But the trouble was ... for Greer ... that Doctor Jenner had. Not in front of Holly, not like Uncle Randall's proposition that should have been for Greer's ears alone, but, Greer being intrinsically honest, it might just as well have been.

7

'He said Yes,' Greer had reported truthfully to Holly, and while Holly had rejoiced, Greer had remembered what *else* Doctor Jenner had said as well as that Yes. It had been a significant ... or had she sensitively found a significance in it? ... 'Why not' ... 'May as well' ... 'Let her go' ... 'After all ...'

Which, added together, tallied Greer, came to ...

'Darling,' and Greer had bent impulsively, she recalled, to kiss the fair head, 'we're going to Bombay.'

The first let-down had been that 'luxury passage', those 'best berths' of Uncle Randall's. Their dormitory cabin had been well down, and it was shared with six others. The second let-down had been those 'pennies to spend', that 'signed cheque'. Unlike the cabin that had not lived up to expectations but after all had eventuated, no money had come to light.

'He's a busy man,' Holly had excused generously. She was so happy she would have excused anything.

'He's always been *busy*,' Greer had agreed drily.

On top of all this, the Australian Bight had been at its nastiest, and Holly had gone down after Adelaide and remained under the weather right to Fremantle. The Good-bye Australia party where most people had at last found their sea legs, when the turquoise blue of the Indian Ocean was making the grey Bight only a grim memory, found Holly too drained and wan to join in the fun. Then after Colombo the edge of a monsoon had struck them and again Holly had been laid low.

They had been scheduled to arrive in Bombay Harbour at twelve noon, and Greer, who had attended camera slides of the Indian city in the ship theatre while Holly had rested, had thought hopefully that here, anyway, Holly would not be let down. She had found the vivid transparencies entirely attractive and had anticipated the lifting smile on the little pale face.

But just to finish off a dismal picture, the weather had worsened once more, worsened enough this time to delay them almost a day, and they had slipped into a half dark port that had made the memory of the grey Bight seem almost a carnival in comparison.

'It's like this everywhere at this hour,' Greer said now as they stood by the gangplank, wishing miserably that she had left Holly below, wishing that she had not thought extravagantly in the terms of exotic brilliance, a brilliance that would lift Holly at last. Brilliance! She concealed a shiver, but she repeated determinedly, 'Like this everywhere, pet.'

'Yes, Greer.' Holly's voice was brave.

'We'll go down,' Greer said. 'See to our things, finish our bags. Get ready for breakfast.'

'Uncle Randall might have heard of the delay and waited back.' Holly was looking over the rail and peering hopefully.

'Not Uncle Randall,' Greer said to herself. She took Holly's arm and veered her in and down.

The other six in the dormitory cabin were stirring drowsily.

'What's Bombay like?' they asked sleepily.

One of the girls kneeling to peer out of the lowly porthole that now at last could be opened up reported, 'Grey and grumpy.'

'Give it time.' Greer felt at least she had to say that. She attended to the bags, went through the drawers to see that nothing was left behind.

Then Holly, taking her turn at the porthole, was calling gladly, 'The sun's through, and it's different, it's exciting! I can see rickshaws pulled up ... and horse cabs ... and a lot of yellow taxis. Little boys are doing the most amazing acrobatics. Oh, what a beautiful sari! And there's one of those others, Greer, the sar*ee* ... remember in Colombo? ... three inches of brown stomach between bodice and skirt. The sari is wearing the red spot of wifehood. And there's a young girl with two black twin plaits and a daub on her brow which would be the mark of maidenhood. There's also a very handsome black car a mile long with a Maharajah at least and with him a

9

young princeling.'

Kerri, peering over Holly's shoulder, said, 'A Maharajah would be driven, goose. This one is driving, but he does look very distinctive, I'll agree.'

The opulent car had come right on the wharf where the other cars had been kept behind a barrier.

'I think,' said Greer, now also at the porthole though barely an inch of it, 'he's meeting some V.I.P.' She regarded the deeply olive-skinned, very erect Indian behind the wheel.

'Perhaps he's the chauffeur to the princeling's father who happens to be returning on this ship, first-class, of course,' provided Holly happily. 'Don't you adore our princeling's handsome pink and orange robes?'

'And that turban on your Maharajah, or your Maharajah's chauffeur,' put in Alison, 'is just his shade.'

At that moment the black glance of the man in question, sweeping the vast wharfside bulk of the *Fairadventure*, by some contingency chanced, then rested on the lowly porthole. Stopped there.

Stopped until one of the girls, for they were all represented now, one eye each, withdrew, rather disconcerted. Greer followed at once, then the others.

'Well, if he's a foretaste of Bombay it's going to be very exciting,' submitted Frances.

'Yes, it's going to be all I dreamed,' Holly said.

Feeling rather caught out in a childish rudeness, not a dream, though the Indian had stared as well, Greer said thankfully, 'There's the first sitting gong,' and hurried Holly out.

They were finished breakfast and drinking their coffee when the message was brought to their table. So Uncle Randall had not forgotten, Holly claimed with a smile.

But it was not Uncle Randall who waited for them in the Genoese Lounge of the *Fairadventure* when they obeyed the message; it was a tall, dark-haired, black-eyed man in khaki drabs but wearing a glowing, darkly blue turban. By his side in full and colourful dress stood a small brown boy. The Maharajah. The princeling. Greer heard Holly, by her side, say it in an enchanted breath.

'*Salaam*, memsahibs.'

The man and the boy bowed low ... a sound suspiciously like a stifled giggle escaping the princeling and being softly checked by Holly's Maharajah.

'Good morning,' murmured Greer. Holly said shyly, happily, 'Hullo.'

The little boy evidently had a hilarious secret. Every now and then he would cup his small brown hands, as children do, over his mouth to hide a laugh.

'Chandra,' the man said quiely, remindingly, and the child temporarily composed himself.

'When the ladies are ready to leave—' the man bowed again, and Greer said they had only their luggage to check, some acquaintances to bid good-bye.

'Please, not to concern yourself over the bags,' the man hastened, and began to bow once more, but, at a laugh, or what sounded like a laugh quickly stifled from the child, straightened to frown on the boy.

A little nonplussed, Greer thanked him and said they would not be long.

There were not many to say good-bye to; Holly's days of imposition had considerably narrowed the field. Within five minutes they were back in the lounge, and being conducted from the *Fairadventure*. Their luggage, they were informed, had been removed and placed in the boot of the car. As he said it, the man waved his hand to the large black model awaiting them in solitary splendour on the dock. It decidedly did not match their recent dormitory accommodation, Greer thought wryly, but then this was for Uncle Randall's show, whereas the berths for his niece and stepniece ...

'If you will kindly enter.' The man was opening the door of the big rich car. At once a little reminding hand tugged at him, and with the briefest of smiles, so brief it barely curved his long sensuous mouth, the man amended, with a salaam now to the boy, 'After the young sahib.'

He bowed low as the child clambered in, rather spoiling his princely effect by falling over the step and arriving on the seat nose first. He did not cry, though, he rubbed the small nose, then, cupping his hands, giggled again.

'Please,' said the driver to Greer and Holly, and they got in the front with him – no tribulation at all, for the wide seat could have accommodated two more with ease. Having shut the door, adjusted the window, the man sat up very straight and waited for the boy to direct, which the child did in a high little voice that broke down halfway in another giggle. Nodding soberly, the driver released the brake and the party set off.

Greer had instinctively put Holly near the driver; always Holly was protected from elements, or the possibility of elements. Not that it looked like wind or rain or any extreme of weather, the sun simply shone goldenly down from a blue enamel sky, yet the heat was tempered by a salt breeze that the driver now informed the girls was a benison to Bombay, which had the good fortune of receiving the benefit of sea breezes on all sides, as it was actually many islands.

'Seven in all,' agreed Holly, rather surprising Greer, for her little stepsister was usually shy with men for the simple reason that, because of her health, she met so few, 'but now the shallows between the seven have been filled in to form one. Isn't that so, sahib?'

Another stifled giggle from the back.

'You sound very cognizant of India,' praised the man of Holly's seven islands and her smooth sahib.

'When we knew we were coming I spent hours reading it up,' Holly confided, as happily confidential as Greer had ever seen or heard her.

'And your sister? Is it sister?' he asked.

'Yes.' Greer left it at that.

'And you? You also studied?'

'Not so many hours,' Greer said stiffly. She was frankly

puzzled at the situation and inclined to be wary about it. Uncle Randall had had a talent for gathering 'moss', the same as he had had a talent for becoming a rolling stone and losing it, but this opulent car, this imposing chauffeur, this princeling child sitting alone in the big back seat added up to more 'moss', or influence, even an Uncle Randall could beg, borrow, or st— She stopped herself there.

'I see.' The chauffeur's voice was still polite. 'Then the pull of India was for one alone, the other just came along.'

'Oh, no,' chattered Holly happily. 'I really think Greer was its first lover. Remember, Greer, how years ago I wanted to see London Bridge, but all you ever wanted was the Pool of the Pink Lilies?'

The car had come to a distinctly abrupt halt for a faultless driver and a perfect vehicle. Greer was aware that the man was looking right and left at an intersection apparently for traffic, but the traffic at this point was almost non-existent, not sufficient, anyway, for that precautionary stop. Also the driver's attention, for all his show, was very obviously not on the road.

'Pool of the Pink Lilies?' he asked swiftly of Greer.

'I was a schoolgirl,' she said abruptly, 'and up to a lesson on alliterations – blue balloons, cool cascades, silver streams, all that.' A flashed and scornful glance at him that brought on immediate, quite as abrupt response.

'*Pool* of the *Pink* Lilies. I am following you,' he said coldly.

Greer found herself flushing. 'I'm sorry, I didn't mean—'

'You didn't mean that I wouldn't understand?' He edged the car forward again, then negotiated a bend. 'Pray proceed. It was only the *sound* of it, then?'

'Perhaps,' she said with deliberate detachment, all apology gone. 'Does it matter?' She was thinking irritably that this man seemed to have a talent for rubbing her up the wrong way. How could she tell that cool dark countenance how a girl of thirteen had turned the pages of a travel book and sat staring entranced at a picture of an old discarded Indian shrine, not its weathered ornate pyramids embellished by rows of cracked carvings of gods, goddesses and peacocks but the calm pond before it, reflecting every detail, yet perforce only reflecting it between its pads of green leaves and its pink petals. Yes, I was lost that day, Greer knew now as she had known then, in a Shrine of Pink Lilies.

She became sharply aware that the Indian was looking across Holly at her, and she steeled herself to look coolly back, becoming instantly aware again of something out of character in this little act of four people ... the princeling, his driver, the two passengers. Why, anyway, was a princeling coming to meet Uncle Randall's nieces? Not that he was really a princeling, of course, her common sense told her that, but undeniably he was most extravagantly and pompously turned out, and undeniably the driver was affording him every respect. Then the driver himself – for all his skilled driving he was *not* a driver. She felt sure of that. To whom did this opulent car really belong, then? Was it all a jest of Uncle Randall's, and since when had Uncle Randall jested?

Holly, blissfully unaware of any undercurrents, called out in pleasure at a cathedral that the driver corrected her was Victoria Terminus, a rail terminus of which Bom Bay was very proud. He said the capital in a clipped way.

'I know that,' acclaimed Holly of the Bom Bay. 'Bom is Portuguese for good and it was the Portuguese who were here first.'

'*Sim, pequena*. Yes, little one.' Holly missed his quick correction, but Greer did not. She gave the olive-skinned man a covert look.

If he noticed, he did not betray it. He waved carelessly across a sweep of bay to what he said was the highest point of the island on which this city was built. Malabar Hill.

'On the lower slopes are the Towers of Silence,' he said gravely, 'but above are beautiful avenues with fine houses. Very pukka.' He gave a little bow of obeisance that irritated Greer because she knew it was contrived and false.

'Is that where we go?' asked Holly excitedly, and he turned his attention on the girl ... a much gentler attention, Greer noted, than the attention he gave her.

'But no. The days of spacious bungalows are gone for all but a very few. Rich and poor now live in flats, though I myself—' He bit his lip, obviously annoyed at something that had nearly slipped out, though what it was the beginning of Greer would not have known had the child in the back seat not called triumphantly, 'We live in a very large house.'

Showing an equal coolness to the coolness he had shown her, Greer said to the man, 'The child's family, I suppose. You drive for them.'

A pause, then: 'Yes. I drive the little sahib.' A smother of laughter again in the back seat.

Holly's brief disappointment of no spacious bungalow surrounded by trees, lawns and flowers slumbering in the sun, walled courtyards in white stone, arcades, columns and patios disappeared in a slow, exciting drive through a market, little children calling, 'Backsheesh, backsheesh!', men selling sweet sesame cakes from brass trays, the big car edging around sacred bulls and sleepers sleeping anywhere where sleep had taken them.

'It's wonderful!' Holly thrilled.

Again the driver's quick darting black glance, a glance that Greer unwillingly found she had to answer.

'Interesting.' Her allotment was intentionally sparse.

They were climbing themselves now, a far lesser height than Malabar. Even though they had left the city proper, almost the same confusion as in the market remained, and the progress was slow. Men still peddled goods, children still coaxed pennies, women with bunches of hill flowers called out, 'Two annas,' then pointed appealingly to their mouths.

'During the cholera,' explained the driver, 'a local proverb told that "Two monsoons are the life of a man." It is not so now, of course, but conditions still beg vast improvement, just as those children beg for pennies.' He gave a little shrug, something in the instinctive movement once more raising that vexed query in Greer. She watched him toss out some coins.

They were approaching compounds of flats that could have been in Australia or anywhere. Greer felt Holly's disappointment and squeezed her hand.

The driver saw it.

'I told you,' he reminded her, 'that the day of the bungalow is over. This is much more sensible, I think.'

'I don't,' called the princeling in the back seat.

The little tolerant smile flicked again and was quickly wiped off. The car came to a halt at one of the blocks of apartments, and the driver got out and snapped his fingers for service and several men ran out of the verandah shade and nodded as he instructed them where to take the bags. 'I won't come up,' he informed them, and Greer commented coldly, not really knowing why she did, 'Naturally, being the driver.' She saw Holly's surprised look, but no flicker at all passed over the man's suave countenance.

'Salaam.' He bowed and went back to the car.

The two girls watched him turn the car, watched him turn his head and nod gravely to them . . . watched the surprising spectacle of the princeling suddenly leaping from his enthronement at the back to sit instead beside the driver.

'He's nice,' said Holly of the man.

'He's an enigma.'

'Well, even that's different, isn't it?' Holly could not be dismayed.

But she was some minutes later when they were led up several flights, then shown into a distinctly indifferent back room. The room could have been anywhere at all, it looked out on a blank wall that could have been any wall. There was nothing at all, unless you counted the humid heat, to indicate that this was India. Even a child crying 'Backsheesh' would have done, a woman selling flowers for two annas.

The room itself, too, was characterless. No exotic touch, simply a room, and a room unwillingly ... Greer had that sensation at once ... allotted.

'It's all we have.'

The voice came from the door of the room, a cold, frankly disliking voice, and even as she turned to meet Uncle Randall's wife Arlene ... for who else would it be standing there? ... Greer knew that their invitation to Bombay had not been seconded by her.

'Randall is not here. I'm going out myself as well. Settle in, we'll talk later.' Green eyes flicked to Holly, and the woman commented, 'Bit exhausted, isn't she?' with more than a hint of malicious satisfaction at the girl's drained, wan looks. Then, turning and looking Greer up and down, not so exhausted, neither drained nor wan, with unconcealed malice, she added, 'But don't settle in too much. Understand?'

She stood a hard challenging moment still looking at Greer, then she left the room. From the sound of steps and the banging of doors she also left the flat.

'What does she mean?'

Holly was standing like a bewildered child asking it of Greer, appealing piteously to her, and Greer's mind ran back to the first time she had met her stepsister and how Holly had stood looking uncertain and wistful, and how her heart had gone out to her.

Stephen had told Greer about his little daughter after he had told her he was going to marry her mother, be her father if she would have him. If she would have him! She loved Stephen. She could not remember her own father, but Mother had said that the two men could have been brothers and that was why . . .

'It's been a long time alone, Greer,' Mother had said, 'and I get so tired and discouraged. But with Stephen . . .' Her face had lit up.

Holly, Stephen had explained to Greer, is not like you at all; *you* should be the holly, Greer.

She had told him gravely that Greer meant the Watch-Woman, and he had asked would she be a watch-girl for his Holly. It hadn't been hard to promise Stephen, and it hadn't been hard when she had met Holly. They had been a happy family, only it hadn't lasted long enough, not for Stephen, not for Mother, not for—

'Darling, don't take on, she just means this room is a temporary measure,' Greer said with the confidence she always practised on Holly, and Holly brightened at once.

'It's not that there's anything wrong with it,' she responded cheerfully, 'it's just that I expected—'

'You expected India,' smiled Greer.

'Do you want to rest or do you want to venture out and find India?' Obviously a rest was called for, the girl looked exhausted, but Greer was thinking all at once on Doctor Jenner's lines. That – 'Why not?' . . . 'May as well' . . . 'After all . . .'

Besides, had they not been warned not to settle too much?

'Oh, Greer, *India*,' Holly begged.

Greer would have liked to have had tea before they set out, but the Indian servant when she went into the hall gave her such a hard look that she did not dare ask. Like mistress, like maid, she could not help thinking. Arlene . . . I expect it's Arlene . . . has imbued those in her service with her own flinty attitude. She supposed they would find a tea-house on their exploration, and clutching her money purse she took Holly's hand.

A street from the block of apartments they found themselves in the India that Holly had dreamed about. The shadow of past magnificence that still persisted through the present-day shabbiness only needed a little imagination to bring all the glamour flooding back again. Holly had plenty of imagination and Greer smiled fondly as she heard her whisper ecstatically: 'Holy scrolls. Peacock thrones. Amber palaces with ebony pillars and ivory frescoes!'

Greer heard herself adding in as caught-up a voice: 'The Pool of the Pink Lilies.'

'Oh, Greer!' A shiver of delight from Holly.

'Yes, darling, but try to take it calmly, won't you?' Greer led the way.

For it *was* a case of leading now. The further they got away from the apartments the more people . . . and cows, donkeys, goats, old cars and bicycles . . . crowded in on them. But mostly people. There was teeming, seething life all round them. Women walking along with baskets balanced on their heads, shopkeepers sitting cross-legged in front of their stores, now and then a man suddenly kneeling in prayer, children begging with liquid tongues and liquid eyes, some cartwheeling in the hope of a reward, a young mother crying '*Chota* baby, *chota* baby' and pushing forward a little brown atom in appeal, traysellers thrusting sesame cakes on them, fortune-tellers, snake-charmers, open-air barbers, pedlars peddling rugs, lacquer, brass and ivory, flower 'jewellery' offerers of delicately strung jasmine, all crying their wares, and, punctuating their persuasive voices, a child's persistent shrill 'Shoe shine! Beautiful shine. Very good shine!'

They passed by a cow looking smugly back at them knowing it had the right of way. Some eye-catching silks halted Greer, and for a moment she stood enchanted, then, always Holly's watch-girl, she turned to check on her little sister, saw her equally enchanted by some delicate silver filigree, smiled to herself and moved across.

As she got closer to Holly, though, she saw that the girl was a little pale, yet that could have been the greenish light cast by the market umbrellas and awnings, dimming and changing as they did the almost brazen enamel blue sky.

'All right, darling?' — But these were the last words that Greer was to speak to Holly for several hours . . . anxious hours, for all at once everything seemed to happen.

Actually, she was to learn later, it now became the hour of the day when the workers not already working at shop-keeping, tray-selling, fortune-telling, barbering or shoe-shining emerged from their places of employment to snarl up the already snarled street. Like a flood they encompassed her, parting her from Holly, sweeping her along in a current of people. People, people, people. Bearded Sikhs, Indians wearing turbans of many colours, women in bright saris, women in subdued ones, girls in sarees, that very provocative Ceylonese garment with its three inches of brown stomach, both men and women wearing plastic raincoats, children in practically nothing, and all dodging sacred cows or sleepers on mattresses or men having their hair cut, and in the middle of it all, Greer, struggling to get back to Holly, struggling even to *see* Holly. Calling to Holly. Attracting the tray-sellers' attention by her frantic calling. The shoe-shiner's attention. 'Very good shoe shine, lady.' The flower jewellery pedlar. 'A string of jasmine for madam.' Then: 'Tell-pardy?' This was from a sesame cake seller. '*Chota* baby.' Another mother was thrusting forward a little brown child.

'Holly! Holly!' Now Greer could not see further than a few yards, the crowd around her was so dense. She knew that she and Holly had taken one of the back ways of Bombay, and she experienced a moment of panic. All at once she seemed in a prison of people, people circling her asking her to buy, touching her clothes, her hair.

'My sister,' she managed miserably, and then did the worst thing she could have done, she opened her purse. She should have had more sense. She knew that wretch-edly and too late as the crowd around her thickened. This would be a basic area, and pennies would be like oil on a fire. She heard the voices shrill around her, and turning blindly ran in the direction she believed she had last stood with Holly.

In her blind anxiety she did not see the tall man barring her way, and even if she had she would not have recognized him, for now he wore no dark blue turban. The khaki drill had been changed, too, to light slacks, silk shirt and cravat. But the eyes, had Greer looked up, were the same . . . except that instead of chill now they were hotly angry. A hand shot forward and Greer was brought to an almost savage halt.

'Let me go! I have to get to Holly. Let me go or I'll – I'll—' By this time Greer had looked up and recognized the man.

'My sister . . .' she appealed.

'Isn't it a little late to concern yourself over her?'

'She was here beside me. I mean I was beside her. I mean . . . Oh, where is Holly?' Greer tried to run again, but once more the hand stopped her, a hard masterful hand.

'Please control yourself,' he advised.

'These people—'

'They will not hurt her. All the same—'

Something in his voice sent Greer's eyes flashing upward in apprehension.

'All the same?' she barely breathed.

'It would have been wiser not to have made her sightsee like this with you, not so soon. If you couldn't wait for yourself surely you could have advised the child.'

Angry words rushed to Greer's lips. What right had this man to criticize? It was true that they should have rested, but when Holly had turned her little bleak face after Arlene's flinty words how could she have not done what she had?

'You don't understand,' she said dully.

'I certainly don't. That girl is frail. Don't you realize that?'

Realize it! Realize Holly's fragility! That fragility around which her own life always had circled! Almost Greer laughed, laughed hysterically.

He must have sensed that she was overwrought, for definitely, firmly, he drew her out of the crowd, the sellers even parting deferentially for him, then he was guiding her ... though it could almost have been *pushing* her ... up a lane, and there at the other end was the large car in which they had travelled earlier with Holly's little princeling. There was no princeling now, though, but a young fair man, he was in the roomy back seat and he was ... he was ...

Tearing herself from the man's light but intentional grasp, forcing herself so abruptly that he was taken by surprise and let her go, Greer ran frantically forward.

For the fair man in the big limousine was bent solicitously over Holly. Holly was lying back against cushions and her eyes were closed.

CHAPTER TWO

GREER struggled with the door handle and succeeded in turning it. She did not get in the car, though. The man bent over Holly looked round and shook his head. But he shook it in a kind and sympathetic way that stayed Greer more than that other person's imperative hand had done.

'She's all right ... that is, she will be ... but just now ... Oh'... a swift, contrite smile ... 'I'm a doctor, by the way.'

'Thank you.' Greer stepped back – and stepped on to the man who had detained her, or had tried to. She did not apologize.

He in his turn did not speak to Greer. He spoke quickly with the doctor in a language she could not follow, though it certainly did not appear an Indian dialect, more – more Spanish, she thought, and at that thought she thought of something else: this man on their journey from the ship to the flat smiling at Holly and saying '*Sim, pequena?* Yes, little one?' Wasn't *pequena* ... wasn't it ... Then that continental shrug of his, didn't it suggest ... ?

The doctor answered the man but far less fluently, less – well, less natively. The man turned to Greer and said, 'We will take a taxi. It will leave them more room. My driver will see to the doctor and your sister.'

'See them to where?' Greer demanded. 'I don't think the flat—'

'No, not there.' His voice was definite, almost flintily so.

'Then – then – not a hospital?' Oh, what had the young doctor answered just now to this Indian?

'No.' Impatiently. 'My home.'

'Your home?'

'Please to come. Your sister is already leaving.' He nodded to the big car. The young doctor was supporting Holly in the back seat and the driver was edging the limousine carefully forward. Holly's eyes were still closed.

A taxi had sidled up to them; Greer marvelled at her companion's quickness in getting what he had said he would. Looking around at the vast throngs it seemed impossible that he could have caught a taxi-man's attention, let alone persuade him to come down the lane for them. But . . . a quick glance at the firm face . . . this man would always get what he wanted.

He was seating her now, seating himself beside her. He directed . . . in dialect, she judged, not that other tongue he had used with the doctor . . . an address, directed it rather aloofly.

The taxi moved out of the lane into an equally thronged but wider lane. It rendered their passage a little easier, though ambling donkeys, goats, cows and cycles still held them up. But soon they were turning into a main street, and Greer did not need to be told that that edifice on their left, looking very much like pictures she had seen of London's Marble Arch, was the fabled Gateway of India. She thought the dock-workers resting beneath it rather less than colourful, but the sea beyond was so brilliantly, almost hurtingly blue that their drabness provided a perfect foil.

They were climbing now, and Greer could see that this area was far superior to where Uncle Randall had his flat. How Holly, had she been well enough to look around, would have delighted in this avenue of fiery flamboyant trees with its leisurely, withdrawn bungalows hedged in massed wisteria and bougainvillea. She wondered . . . and hoped for Holly . . . that they were going to one of these charming houses. But the taxi kept on and up.

Then it was stopping, the driver was getting out to open the door. So the man had deceived her, Greer thought, looking up; it was a hospital after all. She stared at the huge edifice with its white columns and its hanging baskets of fern. She noted the gardens of rioting cannas, sweet peas and snapdragons. She saw golden-hung mango trees brighter still ... as well as shrill ... with coloured birds. She glimpsed a terrace paved in flagstones, tubs of yellow roses against a lavish lattice work. The breath of oranges accosted her, and she knew that somewhere behind the building there was a small grove. She heard a fountain play and a cascade fall.

All of this ... still staring up ... approached from the street below by a lordly flight of stone steps.

'You said it wouldn't be a hospital,' she murmured, her eyes still on the large place. And what a hospital, she thought nervously, it would cost—

'It is not.'

'A convalescent home.' Impatiently. 'Oh, it's very beautiful, but undoubtedly expensive to match.'

'And that,' he commented coldly, 'would matter a great deal to you.'

'It would.' Then she saw his trend. He was suggesting that she would resent such money spent on her sister. Well, if he wanted to think like that, let him.

'It would mean too much,' she agreed flatly. 'Holly will have to go somewhere else.'

'She is stopping here.' He said it in as flat a voice as she had used.

'*I* will decide on that.'

'And how? She is of age, I should say, for all her young frail look.'

He took a lot of notice of Holly. Greer thought this as she reached within her for place-putting words, for this individual certainly needed putting in his place. Ordinarily she would have been pleased for someone to have been touched by Holly, dear appealing little Holly, but not this man.

'Yes, she is twenty-one, but still in need of someone. I am that someone.'

'So speaks twenty-two,' he taunted. 'I have gathered

you are the older sister.'

'Actually twenty-three,' she said coldly. 'Now can we stop this nonsense? We can't afford this place. Can you suggest somewhere else?'

For answers he put the tips of his fingers, and they were cold, firm fingertips, under her elbow and guided her up the lordly steps. Although guiding was the word, as before Greer had a sensation of being almost pushed. Anyway, *forced*.

'Sir,' Greer tried to object. 'Mr—' She was not aware that she put an inquiry in her voice until he answered her. He said 'Martinez.'

'Martinez.' She pondered on it for a moment. But only a moment. 'Mr. Martinez, I will make my own arrangements for Holly.'

'Holly? But that is surely a flower – a Christmas one. A charming name, but that child is no sprig of holly. A yellow rose, perhaps. A temple blossom – you call it frangipanni. But never holly. *You* are the holly. Dark, green-eyed, red-cheeked.'

'You really mean spiky,' she inserted. 'But this is wasting time. I refuse to go any further.'

'Even with your sister in the place?'

'I'll wait until the doctor releases her, pay him what's owing, then ... then ... Oh, *please*, Mr. Martinez, don't start that again!' For the cool fingertips were under her elbow once more. She was being impelled up.

'Listen,' he said, and temporarily stopped. 'It is not a hospital, not a convalescent home, it is a house.'

'A house of this size!' As she said it incredulously she saw from the corner of her eye an eye regarding her from the edge of an ornamental shrub. A dark young orb, with all the jewel qualities of Indian eyes.

'Chandra,' she said. For the little bit of face she could also see was the face of this morning's princeling. So the man beside her, Mr. Martinez, was right. It was a house, not a hospital. Though *he* had said 'My house'. Scornfully she thought to herself that he had meant his employer's house, the house of the parent of the princeling. She opened her mouth to tell him so, but the man was correcting idly, 'No, not Chandra, Subhas.'

'That little boy?'

'Yes.'

'But surely they're very alike.'

'That' . . . a little sigh . . . 'is the trouble.'

'Where is the child's father? I would like to speak with him.' At last she would get somewhere then.

'That, sadly, is impossible.'

'Then the mother.'

'That, too.'

'But – but there must be someone I can speak with. I must explain to the owner of this beautiful house—'

'No need to wait then. *I* am the owner, and I know what you have to say. But until we hear what the doctor has to report on your sister, please to say nothing.'

'*You* the owner! But this morning—'

'Yes, it was a prank. Very naughty of Chandra, very indulgent of me. But children will be children and the minders of them often not much more. I was no more. Please to pardon.' They had reached the top step now and he bowed to her, half in apology, half as a signal for her to go in.

'I don't understand,' she murmured.

'But you surely understand that you are needed at your sister's side,' he reproved.

Flushed and resentful, she moved forward and inward, finding the interior a complete surprise, for, apart from some lacquer and bamboo, an Indian tribute, she guessed, the hall furnishings were strictly Western, elegantly so as well as very old. There was much muted silk, much glowing mahogany, a touch of Baroque and a hint of fleur-de-lys.

'On your right,' the man said.

Greer went into the room and saw that Holly was lying on a divan. The doctor sat by her side and he held the slender wrist in his hand. As she came up to the couch he

27

said, 'It is all right, we can talk, I have administered a sedative. Presently, when a nurse arrives, she can go to bed.'

'I can do that. I mean' ... hurriedly ... 'when I get Holly to – to wherever I can take her.'

'But she can't, of course, be moved.' The doctor's pleasant blue eyes refused politely.

'But she can't stay here. Well, actually she could, but I can't, and I can't leave Holly.'

'I think,' the doctor smiled, and his smile, Greer saw, was directed to someone behind her, 'the *palacio* can run to that.'

Palacio! What was this? Who was this? Not the pleasant doctor, obviously he was English, what he looked and sounded in spite of that previous foreign interchange, but the person behind her, the man who had said 'my' house.

'Oh, yes,' Mr. Martinez drawled, 'there is room enough.'

'Doctor—' As she had put an inquiry, though unconsciously, in her voice to Mr. Martinez, now Greer consciously queried the medico.

'Terry Holliday,' the young man complied.

'For the benefit of the young lady,' came in Mr. Martinez, 'in spite of that happy name, for holiday is pleasant to the English world, is it not, an extremely serious and knowledgeable man of medicine.'

'Now, Vasco,' objected Terry Holliday, but Greer was only thinking 'Vasco'! Vasco?

At that moment Holly gave a little sigh and fluttered her lids, only the faintest gleam of shadowed blue eyes, and the glance fell first on the doctor ... then stopped there. A little quiveringly she smiled.

'That's the girl,' the doctor said.

Now Mr. Martinez was moving forward and encouraging Holly as well. A little dumbfounded at her own exclusion, Greer stood uncertain a moment, and in that moment someone else arrived, a neat, slender, white-

28

capped Indian nurse. In another moment again Greer found herself outside of the room.

She felt like going back ... Mr. Martinez, who had come out, too, had left her ... but she knew it would not be ethical, for in there was now the doctor's and the nurse's domain. However, the way everything was being taken out of her hands infuriated her. She must find this Vasco Martinez at once, have an understanding. Just because he owned the house ... or said he did ...

By this she had emerged to the brilliant sunlight again, but this time by a side door. Her anger still on her, she stopped in surprise at the picture that met her of a small court paved with granite and marble, surrounded on three sides by cloisters of lacelike design, and set in the middle of the courtyard, like a gem, a small but very beautiful turquoise pool.

Sitting by the pool were two little Indian boys in minute trunks. They were paddling their brown feet and sailing boats. They were so alike she had to look at each several times to mark which was this morning's princeling and which the recent eye-peeper.

'Chandra – Subhas,' she proclaimed triumphantly at last, and the two went into hysterics of mirth.

'Wrong, wrong!' they proclaimed in joy.

'But surely you are Chandra?'

'No, Subhas. The memsahib' ... the little boy salaamed politely ... 'must not be vexed, everyone mistakes us, even the grandparents who wish so much to know which is their grandson cannot tell.' He spoke, as Chandra had earlier, in good English.

Grandparents! Greer brightened. Perhaps at last she could speak with someone. Someone, anyway, who was *not* Vasco Martinez.

'Where are these grandparents?'

'Many miles from here. They do not live in Bombay. They have left us with Senhor Martinez, but we call him Uncle Vasco, for him to say which, Uncle Vasco having been at school with our father, or the father of one of us.

Do you understand?' This time, Greer decided, it was Chandra speaking.

No, she didn't understand, but at least she did understand that 'Senhor' if not the Uncle Vasco. For Vasco Martinez was no uncle of these little boys, she thought. He was not Indian, even though his deep olive skin was barely lighter, he was—

'*Sim, senhorita*, Portuguese,' the man who had come silently out to the pool said it for her, said in disconcerting knowledge of her thoughts. 'Also not the real uncle, as you are thinking, but something even closer. I am the godfather of one of these small boys.'

'One—?'

'It is a story you must hear. Yes' – as Greer tried to look indifferent – 'I have decided on that. But surely you knew my nationality before this, surely when the doctor addressed me as Vasco you would know. For Vasco da Gama, our country's valiant fifteenth-century navigator, was, after all, not so far from your own country. Perhaps had he decided against discovering the sea route to India and ventured further south, instead of British, Australia would now be Portuguese.' A little laugh. 'However, no worry. The British and the Portuguese are old friends and Australia is British. So' – a smile and a shrug – 'we two are old friends.' He looked closely at her, then amended, 'Perhaps?'

'Perhaps.' That was all Greer would admit.

'Holly—' she asked next.

'Soon Doctor Holliday will have words to say to you. Until then the words *I* have to say must wait.'

'More criticism, *senhor*?' she dared.

'I spoke out of turn before,' he actually admitted gravely. 'When I saw from my car two unaccompanied young women in this back lane of Bombay I was very infuriated.'

'For Holly.' – Now why had she said that?

'For both young women,' he corrected coldly. 'Do not mistake me, please. Bombay is no better and no worse

30

than any large city. But for young persons to go there alone—'

'Nothing happened.'

'And probably would not have happened.'

'Then why are you fussing and fuming?'

'Because it is not done.'

'In Portugal, perhaps, but in Australia—'

'This is India, and you are very modern and too forth-right,' he stated.

'Is that bad?'

'I could find it undesirable.'

'*Could?*' she picked up.

'If I did not find the two of you quite the opposite to that,' he amended stiffly. 'It is a strange thing.' He had taken out a cheroot and was lighting it. 'It is a strange thing,' he repeated, 'how one sets out with a thought in one's mind only to have that thought altered.'

'You mean,' deduced Greer shrewdly, 'that you set out to the ship this morning with a very adverse opinion of the pair you were to meet, though for the life of me, *senhor*, I can't see why we had to be met – by you.'

'We'll come to that later, please. Continue with your deductions. Almost would I say, *senhorita*, that you read my mind as I read yours.'

'Really . . .' stuttered Greer in annoyance.

He merely said, 'Continue, please.'

'You came with resentment, then you met my sister.' She looked challengingly at him.

'Quite right. I met your sister.' He looked un-waveringly back.

'Since when you do not find *one* of us undesirable.'

'Quite right again.' He actually laughed at her. As she did not speak, by this being beyond speech, he drawled, 'But kindly not to venture unaccompanied in such streets again.'

'Your order or your advice?' She had found words now and flashed them angrily.

'Order,' he returned coolly. 'And why not?' Another

31

infuriating smile at her angry face. 'Why not – when you will be under my roof?'

'*I*. Under *your* roof?'

'It is quite a large roof.'

'It is the roof of a *palacio*,' she flung, 'and no doubt you are its king, but I will not be there.'

'You will be parted from your sister, then?'

'Holly will not be here, either.'

'I must correct you. She cannot leave. I have had a few words with the doctor and presently he will have a few words with you.'

'This is abominable!'

'Before you admired my place.'

'Not as my own background, *senhor*.'

'Then,' he shrugged ... that Continental shrug again that had previously puzzled her ... 'it can be your sister's; you can find a background elsewhere.'

'I can't do that. I'm Holly's watch-girl.'

'Her what?'

'I'm called Greer. Greer means the Watch-Woman.'

'Another misnomer,' he regretted. 'Holly for a temple blossom, Greer for someone who has only ever watched herself.'

'What *senhor*?'

'I am sorry,' he said at once, 'I did not mean that, undoubtedly you are fond of the child in your own way, but when one is strong one is apt to overlook delicacy.'

Greer bristled. Never had she overlooked Holly's delicacy. Astringently she asked, 'Is it such a sin then to be well and fit?'

'No, it is a wonderful advantage, and one, in you, I intend to avail myself of, or I should say use for the benefit of my two charges.'

'How do you mean?' She looked at him in amazement.

'That must come later after the doctor has said his piece. Here he comes now. Please to remain in the garden, it is very pleasant at this time of day and more conducive to talk. I will have tea sent down. Meanwhile you two boys'... raising his voice to Chandra and Subhas... 'can change into your clothes. Bathing is finished until tomorrow.'

Their little faces clouded but they obeyed the man at once. That didn't surprise Greer. He was a person who would demand obedience.

But she was surprised when Doctor Holliday joined her that the medico turned and watched the three, the tall Portuguese and the little boys, enter the house, the little boys on either side of him, their hands in his.

'Vasco the soft-hearted,' he laughed.

'*That* man!'

'That man. Oh, I know it mightn't look like it from where you stand, but—'

'My sister.' Greer guided Doctor Holliday firmly away from the subject of the Portuguese.

'Yes,' nodded the doctor. 'Your sister.' He had found a stone bench under a spreading mango tree. A cacophony of birds stopped as they sat down and the doctor smiled, 'We've put them off.'

Greer did not comment and the doctor did not speak again until a servant had brought over a netted tray and placed it on a convenient stone table.

Removing the net and pouring the Indian brew over thin slivers of lime, putting, on the doctor's direction, a sugar cube in his cup, none in her own, passing small sweet biscuits, Greer waited wonderingly for her companion to begin.

'Your sister is barely over a serious virus.' He made a statement of it, not a question.

'Yes, Doctor Holliday.'

'I think it was a form of myasthenia,' he said soberly, 'a rather rare neurological disease, and one which, if not successfully treated, entails a lifetime of attention and costly drugs.'

'Holly fortunately did not get as far as the paralysis of the jaw and throat muscles,' nodded Greer, very impressed, for the Sydney doctors had not experienced a case like Holly's before, yet this young doctor . . .

'I had met it previously in Manila,' he hastened to admit, 'I was working there in the Santa Tomas Hospital. Having seen it I can assure you that your sister is a very lucky girl.'

They drank and nibbled, then the doctor said cautiously, 'Before this disease—?'

'Holly was frail.'

'She is the fragile build, but that does not necessarily mean—' His voice trailed off. He watched a coloured bird leap from a mango bough to take up a crumb. 'Can you tell me more?' he asked.

She told him how Holly was her stepsister, how when she had come, she, Greer, had been appointed watch-girl, since the child was so frail. Unlike the Senhor, he did not sneer.

'And she accepted you as that?'

'Why, yes,' a little surprised. 'Holly has always known and resigned herself to her frailty.'

'A case of Handle With Care.' His voice was a trifle dry now. She looked at him curiously. What was in his mind?

Whatever it was, he did not tell her. He began talking of his own career. Besides tropical diseases and viruses, he had a deep interest in psychology. 'It is entwined so inevitably with health,' he said gravely.

She wondered what he meant by that as regarded Holly. As he did not tell her, she did not ask. She did ask, however, the present position.

'There's no sign of any recurrence, nor will there be, I think, but she is below par.'

'But that *is* Holly,' pointed out Greer.

'Who says so?' he asked almost abruptly. 'Her doctor in Sydney? Tell me about him.'

'Doctor Jenner was kind and considerate and—'

'And an old friend of the family's,' he finished, 'emphasis on old.'

'Doctor Holliday—'

'Call me Terry, please, Greer.'

'Terry, I don't understand you.'

'Perhaps I don't understand myself at this juncture, and believe me I have all the pride in the world for our Doctor Jenners, but time has not merely marched on this last decade, it has flown. Men have been on the moon, and—'

'And?'

'We'll see.' He smiled at her. 'The question is – will you let me see?'

'See what?'

'See your sister Holly through this breakdown. Will you leave her here?'

'I had rather gathered,' Greer said dryly, 'that that had been arranged.'

'Vasco? Yes, he's a great one at arrangements. But it would be no good unless you were here as well. I've only spoken briefly with my patient, but she is devoted to you.'

'I love her dearly,' Greer admitted.

Another silence. Another marauding bird.

'How can I stop?' Greer broke the silence helplessly. 'How can Holly? We have no money.'

'Her case interests me. A doctor asks interest before reward.'

'Very well, then, that eliminates Holly, but what about *me*? I can't stop here just for her company, I have to do something.'

'What did you come to do?'

'I don't know,' she admitted wretchedly. 'All I was told was a "kind of post". I suppose that sounds silly to you – a girl to bring her sister with her to India on a promise like that. But Holly was so set on India. She lived it, breathed it. And when Doctor Jenner said—'

'Yes, Greer, what did he say?'

'That I might as well bring her. Why not? After all—' Greer's voice cracked.

When she looked up at Terry Holliday he was in a world of his own, his lips were pursed thoughtfully, his eyes stared at the marauding birds, but she knew he did not see them. He said an odd thing, she considered, for the subject they were discussing.

He said as he had said before: 'Handle With Care.'

'Doctor? I mean Terry?'

He came back to the garden again. To her. 'Look, for several weeks at least she must remain here,' he appealed, 'There is nowhere else in Bombay for her to go. There are hospitals, yes, and fine ones, but there are more patients than can be accepted unhappily, and when it comes to the nursing homes that you are accustomed to in Australia—' He shrugged. 'For the girl's sake you must give me two weeks, Greer.'

'I can't,' wretchedly. 'You see when we went out to the flat my Uncle Randall has ... *had* ... he – he wasn't there. His new wife only spoke to us briefly, but I knew at once that— No, Terry, the only thing left is for us to return to Sydney at once, while we still have the fare.'

'That I forbid,' he said sternly. 'I may have no control over you, Greer, but over Holly in her present state, yes.'

'You're not her doctor,' Greer reminded him gently. She liked this young man.

'I am now. Your sister was fully conscious and fully aware before I came out to talk to you. She has put herself entirely in my care. And after all, though she looks a child she is—'

'Over twenty-one.' Again Greer said it. She was thoughtful a moment. It was true, she knew, that Holly as a woman had every right to say what she would do, but – but—

'Can I see her?' she asked.

'Briefly only. At this stage all I want for her is complete – *complete* – rest. Then after you see her I believe the Senhor has some words to say to you. Greer—'

'Yes?' She looked up at him.

'For your sister's sake, agree.'

'Agree?'

'Come and see the patient.' He had got up and was leaning over to help her. A silent servant approached and took up the tray. Greer followed Terry Holliday into the house.

The Indian nurse had Holly comfortable against cushions, and as Greer came in she silently disappeared. Looking around, Greer saw that Doctor Holliday had not followed her to his patient. The two girls were alone.

At once, as always with Holly, the tears welled up. 'Oh, Greer, I'm so sorry.'

'Darling, don't be foolish, you couldn't help it, it was entirely my fault taking you out.'

'But I wanted to come,' wailed Holly, 'I wanted to get out of that place. Oh, Greer, don't say we have to go back again!'

'Darling, *you* couldn't be moved even if you wished it. Doctor's orders, Holly.'

'Doctor Terry.' For a moment Holly was quiet. Her eyes smiled at something. Greer had a fair idea that that something was someone; after all, the doctor was an exceedingly handsome young man. But she couldn't help wondering how Vasco Martinez would consider this. Not very favourably, she thought shrewdly, even though the doctor was a very close friend. Already Vasco Martinez had shown by action and word his gentleness to Holly. Greer remembered reading once how the young fair English type of beauty appealed very much to the Portuguese, and Holly was very fair. Also, to a strong man fragility is irresistible, and Vasco Martinez was an extremely virile type.

She looked down at Holly, at the pale soft hair, the blue eyes, and knew a moment of envy. I should have been born a fair frail lady, she regretted, instead of nut-brown and healthy, and then I could have had strings to my bow, too. But the moment was brief. She was happy for her sister. Only ... a slight frown ... it could be

37

difficult if *both* men continued the same way as they had obviously begun. Vasco Martinez would never be one to stand down.

'You like the doctor, Holly?'

'He's wonderful. I felt I could talk to him at once. I mean, Greer, Doctor Jenner was kind, but Terry . . . well . . . Greer, I told him things I didn't even know were in my mind.'

An interest in psychology. Greer remembered Terry Holliday telling her this of himself. 'It is entwined so inevitably with health,' he had said.

'Terry wanted to know what I did with myself at home all day. I mean before the illness.' Holly was looking unwaveringly up at her sister. 'I had to tell him nothing. You know, I really have been a spoiled baggage, Greer.'

'Honey, you weren't fit enough to work.'

'Yes, but . . .' Holly's voice trailed off.

Presently she spoke again. It was in a serious tone.

'Greer, I feel if I stop here as Doctor Holliday wants me to that I can come out of all this. This – this wretchedness, I mean.'

'But, darling—' Now it was Greer's voice that trailed off. She did not want Holly to lose hope, that was the last thing she wanted, but was it fair to let her build up so extravagantly when Doctor Jenner had said 'Let her go . . . Why not? . . . After all . . .'

Even though the old doctor might not have meant what Greer had suspected he could mean, the bitter disappointment when Holly did not 'come out of all this', as she had just expressed, could do more harm than good.

'I – I feel awakened,' Holly was saying. 'Let me stop awake, Greer. I can only feel it if you remain near me. I depend on you. I always have.'

'Watch-girl,' smiled Greer. 'Darling, I can't promise you until I speak with Mr. Martinez.'

'Senhor Martinez.'

'Yes. But I promise you whatever it is he has to say,

even if I don't care about it, I won't let you down. And now, even though you say you feel awakened, I want you to go to sleep. Doctor Holliday says you must have complete rest. Will you try, Holly?'

'I believe I'm slipping off now,' Holly murmured drowsily. 'Thank you, Greer.'

Greer sat a while beside her. It was not very long before her sister slept. She got quietly up and tiptoed to the door. At the door she passed the Indian nurse who smiled shyly at her. Outside the door Senhor Martinez waited.

CHAPTER THREE

ONCE more the cool firm fingertips were under Greer's elbow. This time she was guided along a hall, up another lordly flight of stairs, then down a second passage. At the end of the passage Senhor Martinez bowed her into a room.

Obviously from its walls of books it was a library, but also from the desk, a study or office. Greer thought she had never seen quite so substantial or rich an office in her five years of secretaryship. The desk itself was mammoth, she felt inadequate seated at the opposite side to the large swivel chair. But, she noticed, it did not diminish in any way the stature or undoubted importance of Senhor Martinez.

He sat back at his leisure, taking out another cheroot and clipping the end. He lit it. A spicy aroma weaved around Greer. He raised his brows, apparently, if a little tardily, asking her approval, and she nodded back. All this time he still regarded her.

At length he said, 'You have seen your sister?'

'Yes.'

'And before that you spoke with the doctor?'

'Yes.'

'Then what have you to say?'

This Greer thought, was going rather too quickly. She said so.

'On the contrary, I am making rather unnecessary preliminary conversation. Rather I should have said at once which room would you prefer, one near your sister, or one, as the doctor advises, on another floor?'

'The doctor advises—' she echoed, puzzled.

'Terry has a theory,' Vasco Martinez shrugged. 'But it is still theory, *senhorita*, and you are quite free to choose.'

'I have not yet said I'm staying here,' Greer reminded him coldly.

'No,' he agreed, 'but your sister is stopping, it is now a medical order.' As she did not comment he asked, 'Did you tell her just now you were leaving her?'

'No. I mean . . .'

'What do you mean, Senhorita Greer?'

'Because of her indisposition I assured her I would not let her down, not, anyway, until—'

'I see,' he cut her short. 'But you did not mean what you said?'

'Of course I meant it. And of course I will remain while she is like she is now, but . . . A pause. Then, and wretchedly, 'But I can't remain too long, *senhor*, and I can only pay you a small amount. You see when we came—'

His face had darkened perceptibly when she had spoke of payment, but as she started to explain 'when we came' he evidently put aside his anger and instead leaned forward to insert a question.

'Ah, yes,' he said. 'When you came. Tell me about that. Tell me *why* you came.'

'I think I am entitled to an explanation, too,' she put in. 'Why did you meet us this morning at the ship? You did not know us; we did not know you.'

'That is true.' Another weave of smoke. 'But we both knew – Randall Perry.'

'Uncle Randall,' Greer barely whispered. Her face took on a pinched look. She felt she knew the story now, that old, old story, the story always attached to her mother's brother. Uncle Randall had defrauded this man and by some means the Portuguese had learned of their arrival and had hoped to—

'Oh, no.' His voice came in swiftly and intuitively as it always . . . and infuriatingly that fact impressed itself on Greer . . . came in. 'I would scarcely have brought with me a small boy if my intention had been *that*, Senhorita Greer.'

This time she did not pretend not to follow his reading

41

of her and she said, 'Then why did you come?'

'I had been to see Mrs. Perry, your uncle's wife. She told me of her husband's absence, then, also, of your approaching arrival.'

'Then you only did a courtesy?' she probed.

'I would like to say so,' he admitted honestly, 'but no, it was not entirely that.'

'Then?'

'Now you have me at a disadvantage.' He smiled suddenly and she was a little disconcerted at the singular sweetness of his smile, all the stern formality seemed to fall away. 'For I didn't come only for a courtesy and I admit it. On the other hand I did not come as undoubtedly you have been thinking, and that is for possible salvage. Is salvage the word?'

'Yes.' She flinched, but she still managed to ask sensitively, 'Was it much? Uncle Randall's debt, I mean?'

'It was enough.' But he shrugged as though it no longer mattered a great deal. 'As a Portuguese business man I was displeased, *senhorita*, but never so displeased that I would seek out two young girls.' He sat if possible even straighter in his chair.

'Yet actually that's still in question, isn't it?' parried Greer. 'For you still haven't said *why* you came to the *Fairadventure* for us.'

There was a silence, it was quite a long silence. Then the Portuguese said rather impulsively, if this formal man could be impulsive, 'Do you believe in—' He paused.

'Yes?' she asked.

'Fate. Destiny. Something at your elbow guiding you?'

Greer certainly believed in the last. Hadn't those cool firm fingertips guided her today? She also believed in the first. She had seen the sudden feeling in this man as he had looked at Holly. Yet she had also, uneasily, seen another face, the doctor's face. She bit her lip, then hoped that the little movement went unnoticed.

He was waiting for her to answer. When she didn't, he

shrugged and went on.

'I thought I would go down and see the young ladies. Yes' ... at a direct look from her ... 'there was a suspicion that they could be similar people. If another wrong to someone else could be avoided, I thought, I would see to that prevention. But when I saw for myself I realized how absurd it was, how impossible. I hoped nothing showed in my greeting of you and your sister.'

'Neither in you nor in Chandra. You still haven't explained that.'

'Do childish pranks ever need explaining? The boys were playing Maharajahs ... didn't you ever play Kings or Queens? Chandra was the princeling at the time, so when he persuaded me to join in, I agreed, but only with the stipulation that it was to be Subhas's turn next. Tell me, did he make a convincing young mogul?'

'Very convincing.' She had to laugh.

'So convincing you would say he could be one?' There was something intentional in his voice that Greer could not understand.

'What do you mean, Mr. Martinez?' she asked.

'I go too quickly. That is to come afterwards. Let us first finish with you. Why did you come here, please? To India? Bombay?'

'On my uncle's invitation. He offered a' – she paused – 'a kind of post.'

'You did not know your uncle?'

'Oh, yes, I knew him.' She knew her voice was grim.

'And yet you came to such a man for a "kind of post"?'

'It was Holly. He spoke with her first. He enchanted her with his Indian talk. I knew it wasn't right, but – but— Oh, that's all I can explain.'

To her surprise, for she had expected criticism, he said quite gently, 'I understand, child. You came thinking it would please her, then when you arrived at the flat— Tell me now about that.'

'Arlene ... Uncle's wife ... was abrupt and inhos-

43

pitable. She was going out. She stood at the door of the room and advised us not to settle. When she left I simply turned and took Holly out – foolish, I know, she should have rested, but—'

'Don't distress yourself.' Again assurance instead of criticism. Greer felt she could not follow this man. But then, of course, the gentleness would be because of Holly. 'It was one of those destined things,' continued the Senhor quite seriously, 'just as it was destined that I go down to the ship, destined that I take the car later down that lane.'

She looked at him curiously. 'You said just now you were a business man, yet you speak of destiny. Also, aren't Portuguese noted for their formality, their conventional outlook? How does a pagan thing like destiny creep in?'

'I am Portuguese, yes, but I have lived a number of my years in India, and India, as you will soon see, *senhorita,* is entirely different. You could go out of my gate now, but little more than a few yards, when a sand-diviner will stop you, or a reader of the palm, or a person who looks into the eyes and tells. Perhaps I do not believe all this, nor credit destiny, but I can tell you this, if India bewilders, it also enchants, it casts a spell. You are never only your own country, never entirely, any more.'

'All right,' Greer spoke with crispness that was an effort, but already the languorous warmth, the spicy unreality that was India was creeping into her, making her feel less her own country, too. 'We admit Fate.'

He gave her a sharp look, evidently suspecting a sarcasm, but he left it at that.

'You have explained, I have explained,' said Greer. 'But it doesn't explain *now*. For instance, how long Holly will be? How I can stop while she takes that long?'

'Because,' he put in before she could go on, 'you have no money. It is that you are going to say, isn't it? Now will you listen, please.'

She listened, then looked at him incredulously.

'Attend two small boys? But I'm neither nurse nor teacher. I was a typist, Mr. Martinez, I liked to say secretary, but actually all I can do—'

He was holding up his hand for silence, and she complied.

'Already there is an Indian nurse, an Australian tutor. No, you are not required for either of these things.'

'Then I can hardly credit it would be for companionship,' she said.

'No,' he agreed. 'But you have not mentioned what you have already told me you *are*. I mean' . . . impatiently . . . 'as well as that typist.'

'What do you mean, *senhor*?'

'The watch-girl. Senhorita Greer, I wish you to watch for me. Well, not for me perhaps but for the grandparents.'

'Of *one* of the boys?' She recalled the conversation by the pool.

'You know?'

'I know nothing. I don't understand.'

'It is simple . . . and very sad.' He exhaled a moment. Then he told her.

'Terry Holliday, British as you can see, Yaqub Gupta, Indian, and I attended classes in England together. I was senior to them, but we were still very close friends. A trinity, you might say. Right?' As she nodded he went on, 'Yaqub Gupta was the father of one of those small boys.'

'Was . . .' She remembered this man earlier replying to her wish to see the child's father that, sadly, it was impossible. She waited now.

'Yaqub married early, as is the way in India. Lalil, his very beautful young wife, in time gave birth to a son.'

'Chandra? Subhas?'

'No, they called him Ayub,' said the Senhor. 'One of those little boys is Ayub. The other names were only given them until identity was established. But where is the identity? And which one?'

45

As she sat waiting, he went on, 'India can be a place of drought and a place of flood. This time it was flood. The little village in which Yaqub, on behalf of his Government, was introducing some modern innovation as a trial for similar development in other villages was to receive the terrible impact of a river that could no longer be confined to its banks. It was all swift and too sudden. Everything ... and everyone ... was swept away that awful time, *senhorita*. It was a dreadful disaster. Then when it was all over ...' The Portuguese spread excessive hands

'Two little boys survived,' murmured Greer.

'Two male minors so alike they could be your English peas in a pod. Right?'

'Yes,' she nodded.

'Since then,' he went on, 'they have developed just as identically. Doctors, consulted, judged them physically as the same age. Unfortunately either from shock or immaturity they could not tell for themselves. And so it has gone on.' —That Continental spread of long slender hands.—'Same characteristics. Same features. Same depth of colouring. In fact—'

'Two peas in a pod.'

'Yes.' It was his turn to nod. A moment while he tended his cheroot. 'But *one* of them is Yaqub's son and one a companion Lalil used to bring along so the two could play together.'

'And *his* parents, the other child's, couldn't they say?'

'He had none. I must explain to you that there are many of these children that India looks after. If a kind person like Yaqub's Lalil wished one for company for her son it was agreed eagerly.'

'But wouldn't the authorities know about him?'

'*Many* children,' he reminded her sadly.

She sat silent.

'So,' he went on, 'that is the question. One Yaqub's son, one a playmate. But which?'

Words rushed to Greer's lips, rather indignant words, but she heard the Senhor out.

'The family of Yaqub is a very highly placed one. I need not tell you the details. After their initial distress was exhausted they were naturally eager to establish their grandson.'

Now Greer felt the indignation in her growing to a hard, tight, angry ball.

'*Naturally, senhor?*'

'Of course. Their own flesh. Their own blood. Oh, but you are thinking of the *mother*. In India, *senhorita*, it is always the male and the male side who is considered.'

'I wasn't thinking that at all.'

He looked across at her. 'No?'

'No. I was thinking it was *not* natural, not at all. I mean wishing to be assured like that. Two children! Two little boys! What difference could it make?'

He was smiling at her. 'I see your trend, and it is very worthy of you. The answer is: No difference at all. The grandparents are, and have always been, most anxious to embrace *both* children. Whatever is revealed, if it is revealed, will never make any difference. It is just that for personal reasons, reasons for the handing over of *intimate family* things, not necessarily things of any value, that they would like to know. Now do you understand?'

'Less than ever. A child is a child. A child is – is *love*. It simply doesn't matter. It mustn't matter.'

He frowned at her. 'It is not as you seem determined to think. *Both* these boys will be treated identically. They will be similarly educated. They will both eventually attend the English place of learning that Yaqub . . . and Terry and I . . . attended. It was because of that establishment' – a little movement of his shoulders – 'that I came in. The grandparents begged of me to have the children with me for a term, to observe them, to see if I could find in one of them what I once found in Yaqub.'

'And you actually agreed to do such a thing?'

'I did.'

47

'You saw nothing – nothing abominable and repugnant in it?'

'What, *senhorita?*'

'Oh' – angrily – 'it's no good explaining if you can't see it, if you can't – can't—'

'Admit that a child is love?' he asked quickly. 'But I told you that you have the wrong idea. It is only to know for themselves that the grandparents yearn for enlightenment. Do you think that even if they did not honour what they said they would do, and such a thought is impossible with the Guptas, that I would stand by and forsake the child?'

'I don't know what you would do, *senhor*,' Greer said coldly, 'but I know that *I* would have nothing to do with it.' She paused. 'Anyway, how could I help? Not knowing the children properly, not having known the parents, indeed not knowing anything about it at all. Not even knowing India.'

'But you might still help,' he said quietly. 'You see there is more to the anxiety than a human regard of flesh and blood. Yaqub was a poet. Perhaps he has passed his gift to his boy. It was a very wonderful gift, *senhorita*.' For a moment Senhor Martinez was silent in memory. 'I believe that you, with your alliterations, with your Pool of Pink Lilies, will like the sonnets of Yaqub Gupta that I will lend to you. *Now* do you understand, even a little?' He looked appealingly at her. 'The parents of Yaqub wish to hand over their son's poems to their son's son. Yaqub Gupta's poems written in delicate charm when he was actually little bigger than these boys are now, for, the parents tell me, he was always a poet. For this tender reason they have asked me to observe, but you, a woman, with a woman's intuition, could observe far better.'

As she did not speak he took out two photographs. '*Senhorita*.' He laid them before her. 'These are the grandparents' photographs of their son and their son's wife. They were taken on their wedding day. As Yaqub travelled a great deal they saw little of them after that.

48

They had only seen the boy as an infant, and infants . . .'
Again that shrug. 'Senhorita Greer, will you take these photos with you to observe?'

She did not pick them up from where he had placed them. She still had a feeling of repulsion. Children were children. Children were love. Did it matter, should it matter, *which* child?

She looked down at last and saw a handsome young Indian, slim, rather thin-faced, finely-featured, eyes as well as the jewel eyes of his race the eyes of a dreamer, a poet. The girl beside him in both photographs was extremely beautiful. She cradled some flowers.

The Senhor was watching Greer.

'How often have I looked at the boys and then looked at the likenesses,' he mused.

'I hope you didn't let the boys see you,' Greer said coldly.

'How wrong you are. They quite enjoy the puzzle. They look at the photos, too.'

'But that's terrible! They shouldn't know.'

'Everyone knew. It was a bad disaster and received country-wide publicity. You cannot hide such things.'

Another silence fell between them. Greer knew what was coming next from the Senhor. A formal offer to her to be a companion to the boys, to 'observe' for him so he could report to the grandparents of one of them. To use her woman's intuition.

The idea still irked her, yet expressed in poetic terms she found it more acceptable. Also, she told herself, at least she could be present to shelter that boy, and by shelter she meant love, who was found *not* to be Yaqub's son, if such a discovery could be made, even though she had been assured that nothing of this sort would be needed, that the Senhor himself, if the grandparents failed, would take over.

'Everything I have said and promised is true.' The Senhor spoke firmly. 'These boys are as one to all concerned – except for that little wish. Well, Senhorita Greer?'

She stirred uneasily. A child was love, whatever he was. Yet refusing would not help anyone. Nor would it help her with Holly. She heard the Senhor telling her what would be expected of her, and it was little more than being present with the boys upon occasion. For this service, he said, there would be a salary.

She heard herself finally agree.

'You would like to choose your room, then?' he asked next.

'You mean a room either near Holly or upstairs?'

'Yes.'

She was silent. She was wondering what the doctor had had in mind when he had said what he had about the rooms.

The Senhor settled the question for her.

'The red and white drawing room would suit you,' he observed, 'and the view is fine. No, it is not really a drawing room, it is actually a small suite. Yes, I will have it prepared.' He put his hand on a bell.

'Where is your luggage?' he asked while he waited for his summons to be answered. 'And your sister's?'

'The bags are still at the flat.'

'Then I will send for them.'

'Thank you, no, I feel at least I should speak with Uncle Randall's wife.'

'You said she dismissed you rather cursorily.'

'But it still would be a discourtesy not to speak with her.'

'In that case I will take you.'

'Please, no,' she refused, 'I would sooner speak with her myself.'

'Then I will send you in my car.'

To that she felt she had to agree. She got up, was told that the car would be waiting her, that it would remain, after the bags had been removed from the flat, until she came down again, that it would then bring her back here. A key was handed to her from a large bunch of keys. Possibly she would never need it, as the staff were seldom

50

away, but it would be there should she ever require it. She put the key in her bag and murmured her thanks.

On her way down she peeped in at Holly. The girl was sleeping peacefully. She had a more relaxed look than Greer could remember on her little pale face for over a year.

Vastly cheered, though still uncertain because she was certainly unconvinced about the rightness of purpose of the post she had just accepted, Greer descended the lordly steps to the waiting limousine.

The big car went smoothly down the avenue of flamboyant trees, past the leisurely bungalows behind their hedges of bougainvillea and wisteria.

They passed the Gateway to India again, and then the route became narrower and poorer, and, because of the traffic, with its endless cycles, goats and cows, because of the sleeping people and street barbers, the pace became slower. Sometimes they had to stop altogether, and then the children raced up to beg for coins, flower-sellers to ask two annas a bunch, pedlars of food and pedlars of crafts ... and pedlars of dreams.

'The lady's fortune,' enticed a sand-diviner; and Greer thought of Vasco Martinez and his 'Destiny'. The word did not fit that Portuguese business-man, and yet he had said it in all seriousness. 'Fate. Destiny. Something at your elbow guiding you.' He had said that it was because of India that it had crept into his make-up, but had it really been because he had looked at a fair fragile girl and known a sudden tenderness?

'The apartment, memsahib.' In her absorption Greer had not noticed that they had reached the block of flats.

'I am to come with you,' the driver said, 'to bring down the bags.' He opened the door, then followed Greer up the front steps ... very different steps from that other lordly flight, Greer thought. She knocked on the door and a woman, the same sulky woman as earlier today, let her in.

51

Greer asked for Mrs. Perry, but either the woman did not understand, or chose not to understand. She stepped back, however, to allow Greer to go to the room she and Holly had been given and for Greer to give the driver the bags.

Greer did not like leaving in such a way, and after the driver had gone ahead she made signs to the woman for pencil and paper. Once more the woman did not respond, and had Greer not seen her glance to the door leading to another bedroom she might have left the flat without any more fuss. But the glance was inquiring, and she turned to see whom it inquired from.

Arlene Perry stood there.

'All right,' her uncle's wife said irritably to the woman. 'You can go.' As the servant went out rather insolently, she said to Greer, 'I see *you* are already going.'

'Well, you did say not to settle,' Geer reminded her, 'you did say—'

'All right, I said it.' Arlene Perry lit a cigarette, and when the little noise of the ignition of the match stopped an uncomfortable silence took over.

'I'm glad I've seen you, though,' Greer proffered, 'I didn't want to walk out like this.'

'Why not?' Bold, hostile eyes challenged Greer.

'It would be impolite, and you are my uncle's wife.'

The laugh that greeted this was unfriendly and sour. 'Well, you've been polite now, so you can leave.'

'Will Uncle Randall—'

'Be back? You tell me and I'll tell you.' As Greer still hesitated, the woman said, 'Cabs cost money in Bombay, I wouldn't keep the driver waiting. Also luggage can disappear.'

'Thank you, but I haven't a cab, it's a private car.'

'You've done yourself well in a very short time,' Arlene Perry said, 'or did you have contacts before you got here? If you're your uncle's niece you would certainly see to that.'

'I had no contacts.'

'Then you've done yourself well.' Again the unamused laugh.

Greer walked to the door. 'Goodbye, Mrs. Perry. Thank you for—' She could not think what to thank her for, so left it at that.

'Are you going straight back to Australia?' the woman asked idly.

'No. My sister was taken ill, so we must remain for a while.'

'She looked seedy,' the woman shrugged. 'Lucky for you that you have enough by you to wait over a while.' She regarded Greer rather speculatively.

'Fortunately I've found a job,' Greer told her.

'So soon?'

'Holly collapsed in the street and this man—' Greer stopped at the sneer on Arlene Perry's face.

'Now,' the woman drawled, 'that's what I call real fast!'

Flushed, not far from tears, Greer said, 'Had we not met him previously I would never have agreed, of course, but when the Senhor—'

There was a sudden silence in the room. It was a sharp sort of silence. Then Arlene Perry ashed her cigarette and said quietly, 'Senhor?'

'Senhor Martinez.'

'You are – there? At his place?'

'Yes.' Miserably, wretchedly, Greer waited for another distasteful parry.

But instead her uncle's wife crossed to the window and looked down on the street below, looked at the big car, looked a long hard moment, had Greer been able to see the look. Then she left the window and came back again. As Greer continued now to the door, the little sound stopped her, made her turn.

She saw Arlene's heavily ringed hand at her mouth as her uncle's wife tried to choke back a sob.

Greer was at her side in an instant, touching her shoulder tentatively, then as she received no rebuff, putting her

53

arms around the distressed woman.

'Please ... please ...' she soothed. She helped her to one of the chairs, put cushions at her back, sat on the arm still supporting her uncle's wife.

Her uncle's wife. Greer's lips tightened. Undoubtedly this was why Arlene Perry was crying. Uncle Randall had—

'I'm terribly sorry to delay you like this.' Arlene was trying to compose herself. 'I did hope to keep it all to myself until you got safely away. After all, it's nothing to do with you.'

'You mean – Uncle Randall?' Greer's voice was grim.

'Yes,' Arlene barely whispered.

'Has he— Did he—'

'Yes. He's gone.'

'Then it has a lot to do with me,' Greer said.

Arlene Perry was mopping up now. 'You mustn't let it,' she said bravely. 'It's enough that I have to face it. I am his wife, so—'

'I am his relative. As a matter of fact, Arlene, his only relative. He was my mother's younger brother, her only brother. That's why I know about Randall Perry.'

'You must have thought I was awful earlier today, you must have despised me for the way I went on.'

'I did think,' admitted Greer wryly, 'that you would suit Uncle Randall.'

'I had to be like that, I had to discourage you girls. It was bad enough for me, let alone drag you two into it.'

Greer remembered their first hostile greeting, recalled Arlene's unfriendliness up to several minutes ago, and her heart went out to this woman. She certainly had made a valiant effort to keep them away from this ugly situation. But she shouldn't have done it. After all, thought Greer, Arlene was now her relative, too, her troubles should be Greer's troubles. And they were going to be. She was determined about that.

'You're going to tell me everything,' she said. 'I'm go-

54

ing to ask your maid for some tea and we're going to talk.'

Arlene recovered enough to insist that *she* would ask for the tea. She did not ring, she went across to the kitchen door, and Greer heard her raised voice, a sullen voice in answer, then an angry wrangle which she could not understand because it was in dialect.

Uncomfortably she waited for Arlene to return. When she did, her aunt-by-marriage said, 'She's unfriendly. I – I suppose I can't expect anything else.'

Shrewdly Greer said, 'I presume by that that she hasn't been paid?'

Again Arlene put her hands over her face. 'I – I had nothing to pay her with.'

'You mean my uncle has left you with nothing at all?'

'Nothing. Oh, I didn't mean to involve you . . . I won't have you involved.'

'Well, I *am* involved, Arlene. How could I stand around and see you left in a position like this? How long has it been going on?'

'So long this time I doubt if he's coming back at all.'

'He has done it before?'

'Yes.' Again the hands to the face.

'Oh, my dear!' This time Greer put her arms right round her and kept them there, even when the Indian woman brought in the tea and dumped it down she did not take the arms away. She looked steadily back at the unfriendly face.

She poured the tea and pressed some on Arlene.

'You mustn't stop,' Arlene Perry whispered brokenly. 'The driver will be anxious to take you back.'

'I'm not going back, not yet. Oh, I know that sounds awful, I mean for Holly, but after all Holly has care all round her, but you—'

'You said you had a position with Senhor Martinez?'

'Yes.' Greer explained it briefly.

'He is a rich man,' Arlene said. A very rich man.'

55

'Undoubtedly.' Greer's voice was dry. 'Otherwise Uncle Randall— Oh, I'm sorry, Arlene.' For Arlene was crying again.

Greer knew it was not the moment to ask Arlene the things she wanted to know about her uncle. Instead she got quietly up and went down the stairs and told the driver to go back with the bags.

'But the memsahib must come, too.'

'I can't come.'

'The sahib will be angry.'

'I cannot help that.'

He argued for a while, indeed had Greer not cut short the argument by going back up the stairs again she believed he would still have argued, but as she entered the flat she heard the car taking off smoothly.

'Quite a purr, isn't it?' Arlene Perry admired. She had been in the kitchen talking to the woman when Greer had come into the room.

A little wonderingly, Greer agreed that it was a beautiful car.

'And a beautiful house. The best part of Bombay. The *only* part.'

'You know India, Arlene. You seemed to speak fluently just now.'

'Just a dialect.' Arlene took out her handkerchief again.

'I want you to calm yourself,' said Greer. 'I know you won't feel like talking now, but later . . .'

'There won't be later. Do you think after what Randall did to Senhor Martinez that that Portuguese would let you come here again?'

'He's not my master.'

'But he's sheltering your sister, isn't he?'

'Yes, but—'

Arlene dabbed, then said, 'You should have gone. There's nothing you can do here.'

'I can help.'

'How can you? Only – money can do that.'

56

'Are you very much in debt?'

'So much I don't know where to turn.'

'Then,' agreed Greer, 'you're right, I can't help. Oh, I have a little. It was to last us until—' Tactfully she did not finish 'Until Uncle Randall established me in that post . . . that "kind of post" . . .' She took the money out of her bag.

Arlene was looking at it covertly. 'No,' she refused.

'But you must.'

'You're a sweet girl, but where would it get me? And that's why you can't stop here, Greer, it's bad enough for one, let alone for—'

'Arlene,' Greer broke in thoughtfully, 'if I return now and take on the position I've told the Senhor I would, would you – would you – I mean as I'm paid—'

'No. Oh, no!' Arlene said at once.

'But there would be nothing for me to spend my money on there. And after all, you are my uncle's wife.'

'It's no fault of yours I'm in a situation like this.'

'But would you? Would you agree?'

'No.'

'You can't go on much longer.'

A pathetic droop of Arlene Perry's shoulders.

'You have to agree,' insisted Greer. 'You must agree. Just say you will. Otherwise . . . well, otherwise I'm going to stop here, and then it will be even worse, as you said.'

Arlene got up and went to the window a second time. Presently she said dully, 'He'd never let you.'

'He?'

'Senhor Martinez. Quite naturally he despises me. That man's wife, he would think. He wants me out of here, out of Bombay, but how can I go? Also' . . . tremulously . . . 'what if – Randall comes back and I'm not here?'

That last touched Greer more than anything else had touched her. Love always touched her, and she supposed that in a desperate sort of way Arlene still felt a love,

57

otherwise she would not have whispered '. . . if he comes back.'

'Oh, Arlene!' she cried.

There was silence for a while, then Greer said resolutely, touched by Arlene's emotion, 'There's no need for him, for the Senhor, to know.'

'But you wouldn't like that, would you. You're fine. You're honest. You're not like Randall.'

'*He needn't know*,' said Greer again. 'After all, it will be *my* money, *my* earning, and if I want to help my own family, for after all, you are my family, Arlene, it is my right.'

Arlene was laughing hysterically, or it sounded hysterical. Greer crossed to the window to her side.

'How could you keep it from him?' Arlene said. 'He'll even question you about not returning in the car.' As she said it she glanced downwards.

Greer looked down, too. The Martinez limousine had returned to the flat. Evidently the driver had been unwilling to go back without her and had simply cruised around. Recalling the Senhor's quick anger, she did not blame the man.

She went to the table in the middle of the room and emptied the contents of her purse on to it.

'I wish it was more, Arlene.'

'No, I can't.'

'You will. And you will later when I have more money. Look, as my mother's daughter do you think I want her memory to be disgraced by my *not* doing this?'

'But it can't be like that, even – even if I agree. He won't let you. As soon as he learns about me he'll—'

'He won't learn, I promise you. I'm going now, Arlene. I'm later than I should be, but I can say it took me longer than I thought to pack the bags.'

'I don't want you to lie for me.'

'I don't want to lie, either, but Uncle Randall has left me no choice. While I can I'll help you out. I'm resolved on that. Just say that you'll let me.'

Arlene put her hands up to her face again. They were still covering her face as Greer left her, running lightly down the steps and almost colliding with the driver who was waiting miserably in the corridor, not knowing what to do. His face lightened as he saw her.

'The memsahib will come now?'

'Yes.'

'Then that is good. We will tell sahib the traffic was bad, a snarl. The sahib does not like a delay.'

The lie was all ready for her. Greer relaxed if a little guiltily still thankfully. She would not even have to utter the lie, he, the driver, would.

She got into the back seat and the car moved off.

The blind that Arlene Perry had moved the fraction of an inch to watch Greer go was replaced again.

CHAPTER FOUR

As it turned out there was no need for any evasion on anyone's part. The Senhor, the manservant carrying up Greer's bags to the red and white suite told her, was not present.

'He is a very important business executive,' he said in that perfect English of the Indian, crisp yet in some way soft at the same time; smooth as cream. 'He had to attend this dinner at the Taj Mahal.' At Greer's startled look he smiled, 'No, memsahib, a Bombay hotel, not that distant shrine.'

As they had climbed the stairs he had introduced himself to Greer as Dulepp, and now Greer, inspired by his mention of the Taj Mahal, asked, 'Dulepp, have you ever heard of the Pool of the Pink Lilies?'

The man . . . he had told her he was a Parsee . . . looked up from the bag he was placing carefully on a table provided for that purpose.

'Yes, memsahib. The Pool of the Pink Lilies is a number of miles and some hours from here. It is a very old shrine that has not weathered as well as others I could relate to you, indeed it approaches ruination. In my great-ancestors' time it was some hundreds of feet high and surrounded by many beautiful gates. It had pyramids embellished with carvings of gods, goddesses and peacocks, the whole being surmounted by a stone trisul. It was a Hindu shrine.'

'And the Pool of the Pink Lilies?' Greer asked eagerly.

'It still exists, for water' . . . he smiled . . . 'is timeless. It is very beautiful. It reflects between its green pads and its rosy flowers the tumbled remains of the Golden Steps that used to lead to the Temple.'

'It sounds very lovely.'

'I am told that it was. How' ... with curious politeness ... 'did the memsahib know of it?'

'I saw it once in the pages of a travel book.'

'Not a modern book, I think. Travel now is streamlined and the old shrine is not included in popular tours.'

'Yet I would love to see it.'

'But I think you will. It is not a great distance from the Senhor's country house. Nor is it far from the home of the grandparents of one of the small boys. Nor' ... a sigh ... 'from the scene of that sad disaster. Would the mem-sahib like Dulepp to carry down the other young lady's bags?'

'No, thank you, Dulepp, I'll check what is needed first.' Greer smiled and nodded him out.

But she bit her lip ruefully over Holly's poor little collection. (Her own was even poorer, but no one need know; it was different with a patient.) What Holly badly needed was a pretty negligée, something much better than the meagre cotton kim that had done on the ship. The pair of them had refrained from buying new outfits in Sydney, thinking they would shop more excitingly and probably more cheaply in India. That could still be true, but with no money ...

She became aware that Dulepp had come back again and was asking her a question.

'It is for the memsahib to say. As the Senhor is absent the evening meal, which, in India, is at eight-thirty, will not be served in the larger dining-room. The question is ... a flash of white teeth ... 'whether the memsahib would prefer a tray in her room or to dine with the doctor sahib.'

'Perhaps he would prefer to eat alone.'

'No, he already has stated that he would like memsahib's company.'

'Then I will come down, of course. You said eight-thirty?'

'That is right. One other thing, memsahib. The cook has asked your preferences.'

61

'That is kind of him, but I'm really very easy.'

'What, memsahib?'

'I mean' . . . hastily . . . 'I like most things.'

'Then you do not insist on an English meal.' Dulepp flashed a smile again. 'The sahib is the same. He likes his Portuguese meals, but he also takes many Indian dishes. The cook would be pleased to make some specials for the memsahib tonight. The doctor sahib is very fond of them. Shall I instruct yes, then?'

'Thank you, Dulepp.'

When he had gone Greer took out and shook out their few frocks. She put Holly's nighties to one side, then added the best of her own so as to make a better show. She eyed both dressing gowns, but could find no noticeable difference in their meagreness. Both pairs of slippers, too, were scuffed. It wouldn't matter with her, but with Holly . . .

She went across to the window, wishing she had not been quite so impulsive with Arlene. Not that Holly would have wanted her to do anything else but press the money on Arlene, for Holly was like that. Still, I must tell Arlene, Greer thought, that although I certainly still insist on helping her I must get something for Holly, too. That beautiful room! That private nurse! And Holly in faded blue cotton!

No bedjacket, either, she went on. She will be sitting up soon, and—

Suddenly all such thoughts were driven from Greer's mind. Senhor Martinez had said the view from the red and white suite . . . it *was* red and white, rich red carpeting, white walls, white bed, red and white striped upholstery on the chairs and the same, in Regency, curtaining . . . was fine, but she had not been prepared for this magnificence.

On a hill . . . only second to Malabar, she had been told by Dulepp . . . the city spread itself before her entranced gaze. Charmingly irregular, the streets, many of them shabby by day, now, since it was evening, became rivers of light. Where the ocean shone, or a river shimmered, the lights leapt up again. It all made a glorious mosaic.

She stood there for a long while, a warm languorous breeze barely moving the flowers of the flamboyant tree beneath the window. She watched a moon come up, almost too gold and too big as it is in the tropics. A handful of stars that seemed so close she felt if she stood on tiptoe she could touch them.

She forgot her financial worries and was still standing enchanted when a maid tapped on the door and called that dinner would be ready in half an hour in the green and blue room.

She called back her thanks, wondering if all the rooms were called by colours, wondering how green and blue had been placed together. Eight o'clock. She had not known it was that late. She took a last look at the harbour, wondering which lights were the lights of the *Fair-adventure* and how the girls in the dormitory cabin were faring, then took a hurried shower.

Besides the shower recess there was a full-sized bath in the adjoining amenity, red-tiled, a bright cheerful red that set off the pristine white of the other appointments.

It didn't take Greer long to choose what to wear, she had brought along very little. Seeing the room was to be green and blue, she decided to go neutral in an off-white sheath. Fastening sandals on bare feet, she went downstairs and was directed at once by the waiting Dulepp to the green and blue room.

She had meant to visit Holly first, and these were her first words to Doctor Holliday who waited for her.

'I would sooner you leave it till tomorrow, Greer,' he said. 'Look in on her, yes, but she is still, and will be for a period, under sedation, and, being only moderately sedated, might make an effort to talk with you. Won't you sit down?' He held out the chair at the table.

Greer sat, saying as she did, 'It *is* green and blue.'

'The room? Yes. The Peacock Room, I've always

63

thought it should be called.'

Again, in spite of the latitude, there was carpet on the floor, though heat was a forgotten thing, for the entire house, Greer had previously noted, was air-conditioned. The old and the new, she mused, the grand old Portuguese furnishings yet this new essential creature comfort.

She looked around at the large sideboard to hold the dishes, at the chairs covered in this instance in blue, green and silver filigree.

'You must see the big dining-room,' smiled the doctor, watching her interest, 'known only as that. It's quite a Portuguese piece – damasks, satins, red carpet, baroque.'

'Strange to have all that here. I mean, one thinks of bare floors and bamboo.'

He nodded. 'And yet Portuguese history goes back for centuries in these parts. As Vasco boasts: 1498 Vasco da Gama at Calecut, then twenty years later D'Alberquerque at Goa.'

'That actually is still Portuguese, isn't it? Goa, I mean.'

'Yes. And only some two hundred and fifty miles southeast of Bombay, so Vasco should feel at home. But what adventurers those Portuguese were!' The doctor took up a decanter. 'Vasco particularly directed me to serve you this wine. It comes from his own vineyard out of Faro, which is in Portugal. But you would know that, of course. We ... Yaqub and I ... used to spend some of our vacations with Vasco at his vineyard, the same as we spent some of them with Yaqub in India, then they spent some in England with me.'

Greer, looking at the wine, said, 'The Senhor Martinez appears to have many interests.'

'He has the capacity for them,' admired the doctor. 'I always think of Vasco as the same robust breed as the Portuguese explorers of five hundred years ago. Certainly the spirit of adventure remains. Do you like the wine?'

'It is fruity.'

'There is prohibition in Bombay. Wines are not easily obtained, though, of course, in Vasco's instance . . .' The doctor held up his glass to Greer, and she smiled and nodded.

'Well,' he said, putting the glass down, 'so much for the Portuguese part of the meal. The rest is pure Indian. I am very fond of Indian food, and particularly Ranjee's. I hope you will enjoy it, too. By the way, Greer, it will be vegetarian.'

A round metal tray was brought in on which a half circle of little dishes awaited them. Curried fresh vegetables, spiced and peppered lentils, curds in many tantalizing forms, all served with flaky cakes that had been deep fried in clarified butter. There were also chupatties to be eaten with the meal . . . chupatties were plain flapjacks or johnny-cakes . . . and small pastry-wrapped packets of cooked vegetables.

Greer enjoyed herself immensely, and asked if all Indian meals were vegetarian.

'Oh, no. For instance, Muslims are meat-eaters – several others. I'll tell you one day. Or better still Vasco will tell you. He has lived many years in India.'

'Yes,' Greer murmured. She was thinking how Vasco Martinez had said of India: You are never only your own country, not entirely any more . . .

They had sesame cakes . . . or tillpardy . . . with coffee and more wine, then the doctor asked Greer's permission to smoke. As she nodded, he took out his cigarettes.

'No cigar? Cheroot?'

'I always feel that they need a Portuguese to do them justice,' he grinned. 'Would you like to sit on the terrace?'

It was glorious out there. The monsoon, into which the *Fairadventure* had run, and which, Terry Holliday said, had only recently ended, had left the trees and shrubs brightly washed by the rains. The enamel blue sky was now dark blue enamel. The beds of flaming cannas were moon-dusted. There was a scent of orange leaves and another sweetness that Greer did not place, but that the doctor said was mango.

'Mango flowers,' he told her, 'are the Indian symbol of love.'

He was silent for so long that Greer wondered if that last information he had given her had started something in him. But when he spoke again, although it was about Holly, and although previously, as with Vasco Martinez, there had been an unmistakable tenderness there as well as any other interest, the talk was entirely clinical.

'Holly was never a robust girl, I think you said, Greer?'

'That is so. When I first met her, when Stephen, my stepfather, first brought her to me to become my little sister, she was a fragile fairy.' For a moment Greer remembered the pale small girl whom she immediately had thought of as Snow White. She said it aloud to Terry, adding with a smile that she had then become Rose Red.

'Yes,' he said a little absently. 'But what was actually *wrong* with her?'

'You mean this last infection? I told you, it was—'

'No. Before. When she was frail, a fragile fairy. What was wrong?'

'Well, she did have a spell in hospital with ...'

'But the frail state, or so you say?'

'Not only I said,' came in Greer quickly.

'I'm sorry, I didn't mean it like that. I'm trying to establish what was actually wrong, I mean apart from the usual, to-be-expected childish ailments.'

Greer could not follow him. What did he mean by 'frail state, or so you say'? *Everyone* had thought of Holly in that way, Greer's mother, Holly's own father, old Doctor Jenner.

Besides not following, she could not give Terry an answer as to Holly's illnesses. She said vaguely, 'She was just not as strong as I was, as other children were.'

66

'And was protected because of that?'

'Naturally.'

'Quite naturally,' he agreed amicably. He lit another cigarette, and, rather to Greer's relief, for she simply didn't know what he was trying to establish, veered the conversation away from Holly.

'How do you feel about your new post?'

'Frankly nervous. I mean if I had a definite thing to do, like nursing, like teaching, I could be preparing myself. But how does one prepare oneself to observe? And then is it a good thing that these grandparents wish? Although I have promised Senhor Martinez I'm still not entirely happy over it. Children' . . . she searched for words, but only found the words she had used previously . . . 'children are love.'

'Yes, but so are families, Greer. Look at yourself. When Holly entered your family . . . or if you like you entered hers . . . the same love sprang up.' He paused a little tentatively. 'Too much love?'

'I don't understand you.'

'I'm not quite clear myself as yet. But I will be. That small argument, incidentally, was really just to defend the grandparents, who are wonderful people, Greer. You in their position would be the same, would do the same. The pull of family.' He smiled rather wryly at her.

About to argue back again, Greer thought of this afternoon and how she had supported Arlene, and how she intended to support her, *simply because she was her uncle's wife.*

'I suppose you're right,' she sighed.

'Don't be so serious about it. And don't dread tomorrow. The children will be bathed, dressed and fed by their ayah, a very efficient woman, then later tutored for several hours by Jim Matson, with whom you should get on very well, for besides being extremely likeable he is a fellow Australian.'

'That sounds cheering,' said Greer. She added thoughtfully, 'This Jim Matson should have been able to give a few clues. A teacher is always very close.'

'He has come forward with pointers. Only' . . . a little chuckle . . . 'the next day there is another pointer.'

'I never asked you about the children's blood groups,' said Greer. 'I suppose that was looked into?'

'Yes. They're the same group.' A shrug.

The night took over. They did not speak for quite a while. Farther down the garden white figures moved across the soft grass, their voices wafting in musical conversation. The whiteness and the cadence, thought Greer, *was* India.

Terry broke the silence. He said, 'Indian nights are very positive, very intense. There's no wraith-like quality in that moon, nor in those stars.' He looked up at the sky. 'Without what such nights should rightly incorporate such definiteness can sometimes be – disturbing.'

She looked at him quickly. The dark blue perfection had disturbed *her*. But what did he mean by 'what such nights should incorporate'?

He was not looking back at her but back at the house. Had he been thinking of Holly as he had spoken? Was it Holly he was thinking of now? But surely such an intelligent man should be aware that *other* eyes looked, too, and even though she had known him very briefly Greer knew that those darker eyes of Senhor Martinez would look much deeper, much longer . . . and because he was *Senhor Martinez* much more successfully?

In spite of the warmth she felt herself shivering.

'I'll go in now,' she said. 'Can I see Holly?'

'You'll find her asleep.' But he nodded permission. He called after Greer, 'Have a good sleep yourself.'

After she had stood a few minutes by her sister, Holly still looking as untroubled and relaxed as she had looked earlier, Greer went upstairs to her bedroom.

She had unpacked, she had bathed, so there was nothing to keep her from slipping between the silk sheets that awaited her. She had never slept between silk sheets before and the feel of them as she had put her nightie under the pillow earlier had enticed her. Now she looked forward to trying them out, for after all it had been a very wearying day.

For a long time she thought sleep would elude her. Everything that had happened, happened once more in retrospect. They were met again at the ship, they went to Uncle Randall's apartment, the episode in the lane was staged again, all the whirlwind things that had followed afterwards. It seemed impossible that so much had occurred since the *Fairadventure* had slipped into a dark depressing port. Wide-eyed, Greer stared into the dark but far from depressing room.

She had a lot to do tomorrow, she reminded herself, she had to earn her keep, Holly's ... Arlene's. She willed sleep, but still the day's events kept recurring.

Then some time later she heard a car pulling up. Then steps. In some inexplicable way she knew they were the Senhor's steps, that Vasco Martinez was home.

She slept.

A little jewel-eyed maid brought in iced paw-paw sprinkled with fresh lime, a pot of tea, Indian of course, a plate of thin toast along with the *Times of India,* and Greer knew it was morning.

Against the pot of tea was a note. It said in almost copperplate writing: 'If Senhorita Greer prefers an English breakfast, it awaits in the green and blue dining room.'

It was signed Vasco M.

Senhorita Greer did not prefer it. She delighted in the cold fruit. She turned the pages of *The Times,* English edition.

After that she lay dreaming a while, staring at the sky that was blue but not yet such an enamel blue, then she showered and put on a floral cotton mini. Thank goodness, she thought, Bombay's heat demanded cool simplicity, no stockings, for at least I can provide for that.

She went downstairs and along to the room where she had dined the night before. Senhor Martinez was still seated at the table.

He got up at once and went to pull out a chair for her.

'No,' she protested, 'I just came to tell you I wasn't coming.'

They both laughed at that, and for a quick moment she glimpsed him as she had glimpsed him yesterday, standing outside of his instinctive authority, his self-assurance, only it was not a gentleness now, it was an amusement. He was almost a boy, she thought, laughing like that.

'I'm Double Dutch,' she shrugged.

'Senhorita?' Puzzled.

'It's a silly thing we say.'

'It is good sometimes to be foolish. So the European breakfast sufficed?'

'Yes.'

'Strange, but I have adopted the English custom.' He nodded to the sideboard with its hot dishes. 'Is that all you wished of me, Senhorita Greer?'

'My directions for the day.'

'You know them already. You please yourself what you do, but when you can you observe. No doubt today will be taken up by getting to know the children, speaking with their ayah and tutor. Also you will wish to be with your sister for a period. The doctor who already has breakfasted has said you are to feel free to come and go to the sick-room. Already I have gone.'

'You ...' Just in time Greer stopped herself from questioning this early visit. After all this was his house, Holly if not exactly his guest here solely through his benevolence. Only it was not benevolence, Greer thought, with Holly, it was – it was—

'I will go now if you will excuse me, Senhor Martinez.'

'By all means. I myself have business in the city.

70

Please to make yourself at home.'

At home! But home, half-smiled Greer, going down the huge hall to Holly's beautiful room, was never like this.

She was pleased to see her sister supported by a few cushions, certainly not sitting up yet but not the inert figure of yesterday any more. The nurse, also jewel-eyed, whispered in an aside that the memsahib was much better though still rather weak; that she had had a light breakfast.

'Please not to talk too long,' she entreated.

Greer sat beside Holly and took the thin fingers in hers.

'Feeling better, darling?'

'Much,' Holly smiled.

'It's nice here, pet. And when you're strong enough to go into the garden you'll be delighted.'

'Yes.' Holly's bright eyes indicated that she was looking forward to that.

'Later we'll do a lot of things,' Greer planned. 'See the Victoria Terminus, a sandalwood factory, a silkworm farm – Elephanta.'

Holly's pale lips framed, 'The shops?'

'Of course.'

Now Holly looked apologetic. Growing up as she had in a family where money was never plentiful, she was reluctant to ask for anything. So instead she glanced down at her nightie, then up to Greer in mute appeal.

'I know, darling, and of course you must have something smarter. It's just while you were lying down that it didn't matter. I'll get some very soon. Bedjackets, too, a negligée.'

'No.' Holly tried to refuse, but her eyes were sparkling. Poor little girl, to anticipate prettiness in bed where other young people—

'Please, memsahib.' It was the little nurse. Her eyes were anxious. 'The doctor said—'

'Of course. And I was leaving, anyway. I'll see you later, darling.' Greer kissed Holly and went out.

She was frowning as she shut the door behind her, and the Senhor, passing along the hall, stopped and said, 'You are troubled, Senhorita Greer?'

'Not really,' she answered.

'Yet you wear a frown. It is not the sickroom that worries you?'

'Not at all. Everything is perfectly satisfactory there.'

'Then—?'

'Nothing. I – I was just in a dream.' Greer wondered what this man would say if she told him, 'I was just wondering how I could get some quick money.' For it would have to be quick by the way Holly was recovering. She could even, Greer thought, be sitting up tomorrow.

'A bad dream,' he said, displeased. 'That is not good.'

'You mean because I will be associating with your young? I agree with you. Little ones should be met with a smile. See, I'm smiling.' She made herself do so.

He smiled back at her. 'It was only a passing thought?'

'I've forgotten it already.'

'Then please to keep forgetting.' He bowed and let her pass.

Greer, wishing she could forget a new nightdress for Holly, a bedjacket, a wrap, slippers, went into the bright sunshine, choosing the door she had taken yesterday, the one that led to the turquoise pool.

The boys were not there, but she could hear them talking as they walked in the garden with their ayah. She followed the sound of the young voices.

They were more soberly clad ... or at least Chandra was ... this morning, in drill shorts and cotton shirts. No pink and orange robes fit for a princeling. Their little brown feet were in sandals.

When they saw Greer they bowed and said, '*Salaam*.'

The mature Indian woman in spotless white salaamed too. Greer spoke to her, but found that although she had been understood everywhere in Bombay so far, Ayah's English was sparse.

Subhas ... or was it Chandra? ... took it upon himself to interpret, but Greer soon suspected that what Ayah said changed on its way to her, for every now and then the two boys would break into giggles.

She was quite sure of this wrong interpretation when the child told her that Ayah advised Memsahib to take her two charges down to the market for candy.

'I can hardly believe that,' she retorted promptly.

'Neither can I,' came a voice at her side, and Greer turned to meet the smiling grey eyes of a man around her own years.

'Jim Matson,' he introduced, 'teacher to these two brats.'

'Greer Winthrop. I don't know whether you know about me.'

'Not near enough,' he assured her gallantly. He clapped his hands for the boys' attention and called, 'Classes!'

With the accepted laggard pace the world over, they left the delights of the garden for a small summerhouse that Greer had not noticed before.

'Feel free,' said Jim Matson quietly as he turned to follow his pupils in, 'to join us. You see' ... a reassuring smile ... 'I know what you're here for.'

'Thank you,' Greer appreciated.

After they had gone she talked ... or tried to talk ... with Ayah a while. It was hard going, but when Ayah took her to her sewing room and showed her what she was making for her charges and Greer suggested a point or two, things went much easier.

Coffee was brought. Greer walked around the garden, running into a cacophony of shrill-voiced, highly coloured birds, who protested even more loudly at her approach, then she decided to take Jim at his word, to sit in the classroom.

Of the two small boys, only one looked up and smiled as she joined them. Chandra . . . or was it Subhas? . . . was too absorbed in his work. A pointer? wondered Greer. A student like his father?

Jim smiled and kept on with his lessons. They were doing Animals of the World, and Greer was pleased to see a kangaroo drawn on the blackboard. 'Does it make you feel homesick?' her fellow countryman managed to insert as he proceeded to the gorilla.

'Sometimes we eat it,' said either Chandra or Subhas knowledgeably of the gorilla.

'Eat it?' asked Jim.

'Yes,' agreed the other little boy, 'but we like Indian dinner better than your gorilla.'

Greer found a sudden urgency to fix up her shoe, and when she could contain herself sufficiently to look up again, Jim had conquered his grin and was on to Fawn. Who knew about a fawn?

'It's a fing on the cactus bush,' said one of them, and the other heartily agreed.

Having cleared the fawn matter up, Jim gave them some written work and came across to Greer.

They conversed softly together. Jim came from Northern Queensland, so did not find Bombay's heat oppressive, in fact it was home from home, except . . . a twinkle . . . it was a much grander home. He had other students, two of them on Malabar Hill, which Greer certainly must see; also a small class in town.

To her question as to whether he had formed any identity opinion yet, he shook his head. 'I sometimes think I'm on the track, then at once I'm right back to the drawing board again. I watch for a flag to be flown, but it's pretty useless. What one of them gains on the roundabouts the other gains on the swings, if you follow me, Greer. For instance . . .' He went to a press, took out a folio and came back with two examples.

'This composition was by Chandra,' he said. 'It's the

story of a boy who had dust in his eye and ... lacking the word for oculist ... called up the "Eye Dentist". Now I thought that quite apt, Greer, even creative. I also thought of it as a possible sign.

'But then on the other hand came Subhas's effort. He really tackled something. He wrote: "I am a mouse. I have emnies:" ... he means enemies ... : "they are the fox, the cat and Umen Beans." Literary talent, would you say? It's like that all the time. One boy one day, another the next.'

'Don't you consider it all unimportant, Jim? More than that even – distasteful? After all a child—'

'I did think in such a strain in the beginning,' Jim nodded. 'Then one day Senhor Martinez handed me some of Yaqub's poems. Greer, you must read them. Have you ever experienced the disturbing tenderness of the Indian Love Lyrics?'

'Pale hands I loved,' Greer murmured. 'Where the yellow roses—'

'Yes. These poems are inexplicably moving. One of them was written still in Yaqub's early teens. Would you like to read it? It's called simply "Bwali".'

'What does that mean?'

'Bwali is the name of a place. Quite a small village, but noted for its beautiful shrine. There is an old Hindu temple and it is reflected in—'

'May I read it?' Greer's hands were trembling a little. She took the paper from Jim.

The poem was inscribed simply as Jim had said 'Bwali'.

Then:

> 'The raiment Bwali wears are these ...
> Saris of hills with folds of trees,
> Sandals of sward, veils of the loom
> Of mango (symbolled love) in bloom,
> Bangles of fern, bracelets of frond,
> Wreathes of pink lilies in the pond

To the Shrine at the top of the golden stairs.
Bwali wears.'

'It's the Pool of the Pink Lilies,' Greer said softly.

'Yes, I believe it is known as that.' Jim got up to start another lesson, and Greer went out quietly.

She went in to see Holly, but her sister was sleeping. She sat by her for a while, then remembered that she had not yet brought down the better of her clothes, so got up silently. Not that they would solve much, she thought unhappily as she went down the hall, that problem could only be solved by—

Almost as if it was a continuation of her thoughts, from one of the rooms she had not yet inspected an impeccable Indian . . . a Sikh, judging by his long beard, long hair, turban . . . emerged and smilingly detained her.

'Memsahib, I am the Senhor Martinez's accountant. Today is the day that the staff is paid. Therefore I would be obliged if you would step into the office.' He bowed.

Greer stepped, but once inside she said, if a little wistfully, 'I've only just started, surely I'm not entitled to payment?'

'The Senhor Martinez pays in advance, memsahib.'

'Is that usual in India?'

The man shrugged his slim shoulders. 'It is India, yes, but a Portuguese household, and as head of the household the Senhor Martinez directs how he wishes things to be done. I have on my account sheet the advance salary due to Miss Greer Withrop. This is you, memsahib?'

'It is, but I still feel I am not entitled. Senhor Martinez has accepted my sister into his house, and although I intend to be in his employ he is still boarding and lodging us.'

The Sikh was very intelligent, and followed her keenly. 'That is true,' he nodded, 'but I still have my orders. If the memsahib would sign here . . .'

Seeing that protests were in vain, Greer signed, thanked the accountant and was bowed out.

76

Up in the privacy of the red and white drawing-room she opened the white envelope. The money was Indian, but she had her currency guide with her. She compared and tallied and drew an incredulous breath. When the Portuguese had said there would be a salary she had never guessed, she had never thought . . .

It was too much. That was her first impact. She must tell him so.

Her second thought was that although she could put what she considered too generous aside and return it, she could now spend the rest, spend it much sooner than she had believed, on Holly.

Happily she jumped to her feet, gathered the money and pushed it into her handbag, combed her hair, rubbed in some lipstick, ran down the stairs.

She felt she knew her district now. Down the hill, past the Gateway, then, being careful to stay in the bigger streets and not venture down the lanes, enticing and possibly cheaper though they might be, into the city proper. There were several large, even imposing emporiums. She had noticed them as she had passed through. She should be safe there.

By now she had run down the lordly steps and was passing the bougainvillea and wisteria hedges, the charming bungalows. She was descending into the city of Bombay.

CHAPTER FIVE

GREER considered the street names rather unexciting for an exciting place. Argyle, Crawford, Wodehouse were hardly the nomenclature for the colour and glamour of Bombay, they smacked more of suburbia, and this hot, spice-laden, teeming place was never that.

Keeping to the open streets she encountered no difficulties, and she interested herself in picking out the Parsees in their long buttoned coats, the Hindus in their folding caps, the baggy trousers of the Pathans. She had learned all this, she smiled, fondly, from Holly.

She passed imposing government buildings, banks, office blocks and squares of flats. These last reminded her, and she frowned, of Uncle Randall's flat.

She looked wistfully down the narrow lanes . . . though did not venture down them . . . with their bazaars and markets, street-stalls and old dwelling places. What she had in mind for Holly, something exquisitely Eastern, something in gay silk or soft chiffon with colours either artfully blended or contrasted, was more likely to be found in those fascinating places. But she had learned her lesson and she kept strictly to the main thoroughfare, and eventually found an imposing emporium with swinging doors, white-clad attendants and an air of decorum.

She was at first amused, then impressed, by the number of those white-clad attendants, for after all, she accepted, it created employment.

One attendant asked her wishes and upon hearing them referred her to another, this time a guide, the guide took her to a flight of stairs where she was bowed up to a higher floor by another attendant. Here, a second guide took over and led her to the appropriate counter. The jewel-eyed girl who looked after Greer brought out boxes of goods and laid them before her. They were nice, but they were what she could have purchased back in Sydney, and she felt a little disappointed. However, she chose a buttercup silk jacket and a floral nightdress, then stopped at that, still hoping she might be able to find something a little more exciting.

After she had signified her wants, another ritual began. The goods were borne away to be collected downstairs. The money was also to be paid downstairs. The girl bowed. The guide led Greer to the stairs again and bowed. The ground floor guide led her to the accounts office and then to a chair to wait while her parcel was being wrapped, and bowed. The parcel arrived and she was led to the door with a bow. A door commissionaire opened the door, then bowed.

'Oh, dear!' Greer said aloud to herself. 'All this for this!'

She heard a low, delighted laugh, and turned round, half expecting Terry Holliday, or Jim, for they were the only Europeans she knew in India who would laugh like that at her.

She was wrong. Someone else laughed. She met the twinkling eyes of Senhor Martinez.

'So money burns the pocket of the little Australian? After the ghost has walked she herself sets into a run. You see' ... a Portuguese shrug ... 'from the boys' tutor I have learned a lot of Australianisms – among them that ghost. But I think I am safe in saying that my clerk has paid you this morning.'

'Yes, Senhor Martinez,' she said, a little ashamed. She added hastily, 'You shouldn't have ... it's not customary .... such a generous fee ...'

He snapped his olive fingers in dismissal. 'That is my affair, Senhorita Greer. But what amuses me, and forgive me, is your eagerness to spend. I only hope' ... a little gravely ... 'it is wise spending.' For some reason his eyes were above her eyes. They seemed to be resting on her hair.

She explained quickly about Holly, how, when she

could not sit up, it was important that she—

'Yes. Yes.' He sounded a little impatient. 'But you must not put yourself also in such a position, Senhorita Greer. I am looking at your uncovered head. It is very unwise for a European to venture out in such a way. I was hoping when I saw you leave the emporium that you had purchased a head cover.'

'You mean a hat,' said Greer rather faintly, 'and aren't you a little mistaken, *senhor*? I'm not a fair lady, not like Holly.'

'No, *senhorita*, you are not your sister Holly.' He said no more, just stood looking at her, till Greer felt she had to say something herself.

'I'm brown,' she babbled, 'my stepfather used to call me his Nutmeg. I mean, *senhor*, I haven't that susceptible skin, I mean—'

The quick displeasure she had noticed he could muster very easily, was now mustered again.

'So,' he said, 'you have not fair hair, you are a nut-brown maiden, but what of your skin?'

'I tan well.'

'You think you do, *senhorita*, but a specialist may have other ideas. Had you shown perception you would have seen that though this is their country, and their skins naturally adapted, the Indian woman nonetheless throws aside her head veil only where there is shade not heat. Apart from exhaustion, the sun can do much skin damage. Come, we must rectify this at once.'

'But—'

'Yes, child?'

'I didn't want to spend that money. I mean, although I have purchased what was needed for Holly, it wasn't quite what I wanted, and I – well, I—'

'But surely, *senhorita*,' he said indulgently, and had she looked up she would have seen a twinkle in his eyes, 'there would be enough for both of you. I mean presumably you would not be bankrupt, depleted, upon your arrival here.'

80

Silence.

'*Would* you, *senhorita*?'

No, thought Greer, I wasn't, it wasn't much I had, but I still had prudently put a little aside for us, only when Arlene came on the scene . . .

Suddenly she realized he was laughing softly. 'So,' he said, 'money *does* burn in your pocket. You spent everything on your trip across. A typical girl! Come, spend more now.' He turned her back through the swinging doors.

Once more they went through the ritual of the attendants, but the 'head cover' he insisted upon, a green-lined topee, turned out to be so ridiculously cheap that Greer almost cried aloud with relief.

'So,' he said again, 'it was not such an extraction after all, now was it?' They were out on the street by now, and he put cool olive fingertips under her arm and led her down one of the narrow lanes she had coveted, stopping at a small eastern store.

'This place is reliable, Senhorita Greer, you will be shown good authentic stuff yet not charged a devilish rate. It is also clean.'

They went in. At once cool drinks arrived. Then a woman displayed embroidered *cholis*, which were blouses to wear under a sari, but which would make, and Greer recognized it at once, excellent jackets to sit up in bed in a climate like Bombay's.

Delighted with her purchases because she knew Holly would be delighted with them, relieved because they did not exhaust her pay packet, she turned grateful eyes to the Senhor.

'Thank you. They're just what I wanted for Holly.'

'And for you yourself? What do you want for Senhorita Greer?'

'Well, nothing, really, I mean . . .' She meant there *were* things, for a woman there are always things, but until Arlene was helped . . . Her grasp on her pay packet tightened resolutely.

81

'I see you have taken to heart my banter because of your inability to hold money,' he teased. 'Please not to be annoyed with me. Come, I will repent over a cup of Indian tea.'

Though the tea was certainly Indian, it was taken at a very European hotel – Green's. Almost Victorian, cool, vast, relaxing. Before the tea they both had a long frosted glass of *limbu pani*, fresh lime-juice. Their thirsts slaked by the refreshing drink, they sat back and leisurely nibbled at sweet biscuits and sipped the hot fragrant tea.

Greer rather had dreaded that the Portuguese would adopt his bantering mood again, upbraid her for being something of a spendthrift, for she felt, because of Arlene, that such a conversation could tread on dangerous ground. But he talked instead about Bombay . . . about all India . . . and soon she forgot her qualms in her complete fascination in what he had to relate.

His conversation was varied, it ran a complete gamut. From crows whose call of Ram-ram as they collected street garbage quicker than the dustman could to Indian houses with samplers on the wall, most often reading: 'What is a home without order?' To Indian coffee palaces . . . he said *palacois* . . . where in Urdu, Hindu, Hindustani, English, Punjabi, Bengali . . . others . . . many things were argued, most important of all, perhaps . . . and now the Senhor started another gamut . . . the discussion of marriage.

It was a very sober thing, marriage. It was considered an obligation that a man dispose of his daughters. As much money as he could afford, or jewels, were put aside for this essential business.

'It certainly sounds like a business,' Greer said disapprovingly.

The Senhor did not answer, and she supposed that in the Portuguese circles his forebears had moved it would be a business also. Social position, monetary expectations, status, lineage. She wondered if it would be a business still with him, for he was very much, in spite of the fact that he had said he moved around a great deal, that he had been partly educated in England, *Portuguese.*

'Well, perhaps,' he admitted of her disparagement, 'but not always.'

He told her about a fraudulent action. A family had made a good match for their son by pretending to be rich people. They had borrowed, in the owner's absence, a fine villa, presented the young man in dazzling colours. At length a dowry had been agreed upon on the bride's side, a very good one, and the kill had been made by the gleeful parents of the groom.

As Greer's face tightened at 'kill' the Senhor said, 'But something one did not expect happened, Senhorita Greer. These two young people fell in love. So all was well, even though the horoscopes had been tampered with.'

'Horoscopes?'

'Of course. Always a horoscope must be exchanged first. Now, what are you, Senhorita Greer? For if you are a Leo or—'

'How ridiculous,' demeaned Greer, her cheeks flushed.

He laughed at her and said, 'No matter, I will ask my accountant, because, for the records, he will be requiring from you your date of birth.'

'And Holly's?' she said abruptly.

'I would not need your sister's,' he mused.

No, thought Greer, it would be like that Indian and his bride ... it wouldn't matter because there was love. Or, at this stage, the tenderness that precedes love.

'Shall we go now?' the Senhor was asking. He had risen and he leaned over and helped Greer to her feet. His fingers were firm as always under her elbow.

Returning in the car that the Senhor had awaiting him, Greer spoke about her attendance in the schoolroom this morning, her talk with the boys' tutor.

'He showed me a poem of Yaqub's,' she said shyly.

' "Bwali"?'

'Yes.'

'You liked it?'

'Oh, yes.' That was all she could find to say. Suddenly she was turning the pages of that travel book all those years ago and looking with wonderment ... that had never left her ... at a picture of a Hindu shrine and beneath it a looking-glass pond set with rosy flowers. 'Pool of the Pink Lilies.' She was not aware that she whispered it aloud until he nodded at her.

'Yes,' he said quietly. 'It is your dream to come true, for it *was* a dream, was it not, Senhorita Greer, and never just an alliteration?'

'A dream,' she said, surprising herself with the admission.

'And of course you will see it. It is never a Taj Mahal. Never, either, the Tank of the Golden Lotus which is at Madura and a very famous shrine.' He took out his cheroots. 'Tell me, *senhorita*,' he asked, changing the subject, 'even though it is early to judge as yet, did you notice anything at all during your attendance with the boys?'

'No,' said Greer, but she couldn't contain a giggle, and seeing his inquiring glance she told him about the 'gorilla' for dinner, the 'fawn' that grew on a cactus.

To her relief ... otherwise she would have felt ridiculous ... he laughed, too, laughed heartily. So he had a sense of humour, this Portuguese. 'No sign there yet,' he stated.

They were climbing the hill now, passing the hedges of wisteria and bougainvillea. Greer found herself looking forward to seeing Holly's pleased little face as she tumbled the goodies she had bought for her on to the bed.

The big car curved to a halt and the driver got out to hold open the door. Clutching her purchases, Greer got out.

The Senhor was not far behind her, but he went back to the car again to give the driver some direction.

84

Hesitating whether to run ahead or wait for him, Greer heard the soft but penetrating voice. 'Madame ... Madame!' After Senhorita, after Memsahib, it caught Greer's attention, and she turned.

Not on the property, which was unfenced yet marked by bordering palms, but near enough to the edge of it to be almost there, stood an Indian woman, her veil drawn over her head.

'Madame!' she called urgently again.

Still Greer would have gone on, for she knew by now the inadvisability of committing oneself to these appealing people without thinking first; more good, she had learned, could be done in other ways. But she didn't go on. Something in the tone of that 'Madame' stayed her, something sulky somehow, something evasive, insolent. She looked at the woman and the woman looked back at her, looked narrowly, a little challengingly. Remindingly. Reminding Greer they had met before. Met ... at Uncle Randall's flat. Why – why, this woman was Arlene's maid, the unwilling, unfriendly maid who none the less stayed on, because Arlene had admitted that she had not been paid.

'Madame, a note.' In her recognition Greer had moved to the footpath and now the woman put a folded paper quickly in her hand.

Almost at once the Senhor spoke peremptorily, rather angrily by the tone of his voice, though Greer, because he spoke in dialect, could not understand what he said. Before he had finished speaking the woman had hurried away.

Senhor Martinez finished what he had to say to Greer, though, and it was terse and displeased.

'I do not wish you to encourage these people, *senhorita*. You may feel sorry for them, but believe me, and believe the many reputable Indians who advise what I say now, it is not the right way. Independence, stability, pride, those are the things that are wished for them, not humiliating charity. What did you give her?'

'Nothing. She did not ask me for anything.' That was true enough, Greer thought.

It did not satisfy the man. 'You mean she was simply standing there and you went across to her?'

'Yes.' That was not true, but what more under the circumstances could she say?

He stood incredulous for a while, all the time his eyes raking at her, searching for a truth.

'Did she give anything to you?'

'Of course not.' With the note tight in her hand Greer uttered the lie angrily, hoping that he would be rebuffed by her apparent resentment.

He was not rebuffed, but he did drop his questioning.

'Come,' he said, and led the way up the lordly steps.

The note burned the pocket in which Greer had slipped it, but it was hours before she could stop the burning.

First Holly delayed her. Her bedroom door had been opened to entertain the patient by passers-by in the hall, for evidently she was well enough now to be permitted entertainment, and she called out happily, 'Oh, Greer!'

'Darling!' The note was pushed further into the pocket, and Greer went into the room, tumbling the parcels, as she had planned, on to the bed.

But in the delight of Holly's delight she temporarily forgot her urgency. First of all she showed her sister the more formal purchases, and then the quite delicious *cholis*, all in mouth-watering colours, one featuring the wild gold lilies that were offered for two annas a bunch, one the dusky bloom of an evening sky with incense rising in smoky curls, and the eternal ... it seemed ... mango flowers, the love symbol, in green-gold.

'They're beautiful, all of them,' enthused Holly, but she immediately put on the last. As she fastened up the final button the Senhor came to the door and asked could he enter. His eyes at once took in the mango blossom, and he smiled gently at Holly.

'So,' he said. That was all. 'So.' Greer stood waiting for Holly to say something back to him, inquire what he meant, but Holly just lay there in her pretty *choli* and smiled at the Portuguese.

'I'll go upstairs.' Greer turned slowly, then remembered her note and stepped out more quickly.

'*Senhorita.*' The Senhor delayed her progress. 'The children are at the pool. I always find it a more opportune moment to observe them when they are at play. They are relaxed then, unconscious of supervision. Perhaps you could watch now, unless' . . . a slight sharpness in his voice . . . 'you have other things to do.'

'Of course not.' Greer, relieved of her parcels and bag, went untrammelled out to the pool. No qualms about the note, it still lay hidden in her pocket.

The children were sailing their boats and having a grand time. Again, as when she had joined Holly, Greer forgot what had burned her. She laughed as one of the boys' boats foundered . . . but the next minute was not laughing. Chandra . . . or was it Subhas? . . . was coughing and spluttering and getting out of his depth as he endeavoured to save the boat.

She hauled both the boat and its captain back into shallow waters, then looked a little incredulously at the child.

'You could have drowned. Why did you let yourself flounder like that?' In case he did not understand 'flounder' she did the actions.

'The water was in my nose, I wanted to cough.'

'Of course. But you should have taken a deep breath before you went under after your boat. Chandra . . . or is it Subhas? . . . but it doesn't matter, anyway, can't you swim?'

'No. And he can't, too.'

'Can't swim?' But she had seen little brown bodies in the streams obviously as at home as on their legs in the streets.

'It is not to be,' said one of the boys.

'The grandparents of one of us has said so,' added the other.

'But this is terrible. Don't you *want* to swim?'

'Yes, then I can get my boat when it floats away and not get water in my nose.'

'And not get drowned,' said the other helpfully.

'But we still must not swim,' they both chorused, 'it is the orders of the grandparents of cne of us.'

'That is true.' The Senhor was now standing beside Greer. He waited until the children returned to their launching activities, then said in a quiet voice, 'I know that that to an Australian is incomprehensible, but it still is the wish of those two unhappy people. Water took from them their dearest possessions, now they are nervous it can happen again.'

'It nearly happened just now,' said Greer bluntly; she was still a little unnerved by the incident. 'Can't these grandparents be told that the best way to avoid tragedy is to be prepared to handle it?'

'I agree entirely with you, Senhorita Greer, and that is why . . .' He looked at the turquoise pool and made an indicative gesture at it. 'It was not always here,' he stated, 'in fact I only had it installed when I agreed to accept the children for a term.'

'You mean you felt the importance, too?' Greer said eagerly. 'Felt it sufficiently to—'

'To do something that was forbidden? Yes. Please not to think, Senhorita Greer, that at any time by the pool these boys have not been guarded. Eyes had been on them and at the first signs of trouble—'

'But still they can't swim.'

'I have been making haste slowly. Is that right, please? Both of these children have had a very bad experience with water. I wanted them to get the friendly feel of it, the liking for it before they went a step farther.'

'You were wise, Senhor Martinez, but don't you think they are ready now? I mean even though eyes, as you say, have watched them, children are slippery little customers, they can elude care very successfully and, sadly, often tragically.'

'Again I agree entirely with you.' A pause. 'When can you start?'

'I, *senhor*?'

'Why not? That is, of course, after I speak with the grandparents. What better a time to "observe" than at a time when children are at their most natural, and that is swimming. Though perhaps' . . . a little disbelieving smile . . . 'you are not in a position to teach them.'

'I can swim,' nodded Greer. Then, at a little knowing nod from him, 'Why did you suppose so in such a confident manner, *senhor*?'

'The nutbrown maid,' he reminded her. 'You may not be a fair lady, as you have been at pains to tell me, but your skin still shows signs of many hours of sun in spite of its warmer-hued base. There are also five freckles.' As she stood a little embarrassed by his scrutiny, he said seriously, 'Will you instruct these children later, *senhorita*?'

'I'm no expert.'

'Just sufficient to keep a small body afloat. Greater proficiency might oblige me to confess to the grandparents that they have on their hands a prodigy,' he laughed.

Greer laughed, too, then agreed. Indeed, the idea of joining the boys in the turquoise pool was a very alluring one. She was glad she had brought her swimming things with her from Australia – several sets, since one needed them on board ship.

'Then that is very good,' Senhor Martinez said. 'When they become more confident we will all have a day at the beach . . . oh, yes, there are some splendid beaches on the coast. But first the crawl . . . am I right, *senhorita*?'

'The crawl comes long afterwards,' she corrected, 'indeed it is the finished stroke, and if either of the boys masters it then he will indeed end up a small prodigy.'

'You tell a man of the sea what is first and what is last,'

he pretended to frown, 'for indeed the Portuguese are that. Our country was attending to the waves many centuries before you were.'

'That was only because we hadn't been heard of,' she bantered back, and they both laughed.

The boys, sensing an adult frolic, joined merrily in by splashing water, and Greer, reaching in her pocket for a handkerchief to dry herself while the Senhor called for order, felt the note again. It changed everything.

She waited around, barely hiding her impatience, until the Senhor called the boys out of the water and their ayah took over. Then at last she ran up the stairs to her room.

She shut the door behind her and took out the letter and unfolded it. It was, as she had guessed, from Arlene, though Uncle Randall's wife had cautiously not signed her name.

It said simply but urgently: 'Can you come?'

When Dulepp inquired as to whether the memsahib would dine downstairs tonight, Greer said no, that she would have a tray and eat with her sister in the sickroom. She did not know whether the nurse would approve of this, but it seemed to her as well as a way of being with Holly a way of knowing whether Senhor Martinez had left the house, the sick-bay being so centrally situated so that every coming and going could be seen and heard. It had been chosen for this. Doctor Holliday had told her he considered that unless a patient was seriously ill and in need of absolute quiet, diversion was a very desirable thing.

The little nurse did not mind, and Holly said her invalid diet tasted twice as nice with Greer to talk to. She was still elated over her new things, and chattered so much that she grew tired and the nurse gave Greer some meaningful looks.

But still Greer sat on. She felt sure that the Portuguese business man would be going out again, then when he went ...

She was right. Through a crack supplied by the not-quite-closed door she saw him ascend the stairs after dinner, then soon afterwards descend them again.

He was in evening dress, and for a moment his splendour took away her breath. He stood briefly clipping a cheroot, and she watched him through the small opening. Where was he going? she wondered. With whom? She glanced down at Holly, drifting off to sleep now, and hoped uneasily that those gentle looks of the Portuguese were not giving her little sister any foolish ideas. That tycoon was not for a naïve girl like Holly.

She was glad of the evening splendour, however, even though it gave her an odd pang, for it meant that he would be away for the night, and what she had to do would not take long.

She waited till she heard the big car move off, then she kissed Holly goodnight, Holly not noticing, then took up the handbag she had left there earlier and went unobtrusively out of the house and down the front steps.

She was not frightened, not even the slightest bit nervous. The hill where the house was situated was a very exclusive area, no harm could come to her here, she had only to wait for a taxi, and in such a privileged area taxis should pass quite frequently.

Perhaps it was the time of evening, or perhaps the hill residents used their own cars, but it was quite a while before she hailed one. She had moved down from the big house so as not to be seen, and though the wisteria and bougainvillea hedges were very attractive by day, by night they were rather too concealing. She was relieved when the cab pulled up and the driver opened the door. She told him the address of the flat.

After some fifteen minutes she began to worry. She felt sure that the journey had not taken this long the last time. She peered out of the window and was reassured by public buildings, lights, people. I'm not being kidnapped, anyhow, she tried to smile.

Another five minutes and another peep out of the window, and still buildings, lights, people. The *same* buildings, lights, people?

The landmark of the Victoria Railway Station caught her eye; she could not mistake having seen that before. She called out, 'Driver, you're doing the same route again. Please take me to that address at once.'

The driver turned and explained plausibly that it was dangerous taking Memsahib down the side lanes, that in keeping to the main ways he had only been thinking of Memsahib's safety.

'Very well, but don't think about it a third time,' warned Greer.

There must have been a certain note in her voice . . . or at least an acceptance in the man that no extra money would be forthcoming, for within a few minutes they pulled up at the flat. Greer paid what she was asked, not feeling capable of argument, but told the taxi off.

She went up the stairs. Arlene must have been watching for her, for she opened the door at once.

'Oh, Greer, I'm so glad you could come. Not that you can do any good . . . I'm not expecting that . . . it's just that I want you to know.'

'What is it, Arlene?'

'More trouble.' Arlene turned her back on Greer. Greer saw the shuddering of her shoulders.

'Please tell me.' Greer crossed to her side. 'At least if I can't help you, I can listen. Then why can't I help, Arlene?'

For answer Arlene whispered an amount of money that explained everything. 'I've given up trying any more, Greer,' she sobbed, 'it's just too much. After all' . . . a pathetic look at Greer . . . 'what can further shame mean to me now? But I felt I had to tell you . . . prepare you. That is, if one *can* be prepared for a thing like this.' Another burst of sobs.

'A debt, Arlene?'

'That's the kinder word. Yes, Greer. Only *this* person

won't be like your Portuguese.'

'He's not that.'

A quick sharp look that Greer did not notice. 'I really meant a superior person, Greer. One who doesn't . . . who wouldn't . . . Oh, no, this one will want his pound of flesh. There'll be publicity.' A shudder. 'Oh, I'm terribly sorry for you, Greer. Not for myself, I think I'm beyond feeling now. But I've come to know you, and it's made everything different. Before you arrived I thought of you as just Randall's relation. Now . . .' Arlene spread her ringed fingers.

'Thank you for telling me,' Greer said dully. The amount Arlene had whispered had considerably shocked her. 'There's nothing, as you said, that I can do, of course.'

'Nothing.' Arlene was watching her closely, wetting her lips as though preparing to say something. But she must have changed her mind, for she waited instead for Greer to make the first move.

'I told you last time, Arlene,' said Greer, 'that I would help you from my salary.'

'Yes, and it was sweet of you, but of course it will be a few weeks yet before you receive any payment, and even then . . .' A despairing shrug.

'But I've been paid in advance,' Greer came in eagerly. 'Also it was such a generous rate I was astounded. I had to purchase some things for Holly, but if what I have here can help . . .'

Had she been able to see Arlene's face she would have read that this was not, or rather the amount was not, what Arlene wanted, but Arlene could bide her time, and if a hand-out was available . . .

'I couldn't. You've done enough,' Arlene objected.

'Not nearly enough, from what you tell me,' sighed Greer. She had a brainwave. 'Perhaps you could appease this person for a while. Advance just part of the debt.' She said debt resolutely; she could not make it fraud. 'You could tell him . . . promise him . . .'

'That there'll be more?' put in Arlene quickly. 'Yes, I

think I see what you mean. Oh, you are a dear girl! But how *can* I? How *can* I, Greer?' As she was saying it her eyes were raking the notes that Greer had put down.

Somewhere a clock chimed, and Greer knew she must not wait any longer.

'The taxi that brought me charged a shocking amount,' she told her uncle's wife.

'You have to outsmart them.' There was a contemptuous note in Arlene's voice. She must have heard it herself, for she covered up hurriedly, 'Which a girl like you couldn't bring herself to do. Go to the end of the street when you return, there are more taxis there, and let the driver know what you're about.'

'I'll do that. I'll come again, Arlene. But don't send your woman if you can help. Senhor Martinez . . . well . . . that is . . .' She stammered into silence.

Arlene was watching her, listening to her. A little smile played round her mouth.

'I understand, dear. Now I think you'd better go. Do as I said and try the end of the street. And Greer, *thanks.*'

Greer was out of the building again, hurrying to the busier road. As Arlene had said, there were numbers of taxis. In a few minutes she had chosen a reputable-looking one and got in. But before they moved off, she briefed the driver.

'I do not want to be taken by a roundabout way. I want to get there by the shortest route. I will pay what is due, and something for you yourself, but I will not be overcharged as I was when I came across. Do you understand?'

'I understand, memsahib.' The driver, older than the driver who had brought her to the flat, looked a little hurt. Well, so long as he gets me there I don't care, Greer thought.

. . . But she was to care. And to wish she hadn't lectured him.

Arriving at the hill house, the driver asked to see the sahib of the house in order to tell the sahib that he had brought the memsahib back safely.

'There is no need.'

'There is every need, memsahib, I am an honourable man, I wish to see the sahib's face and assure him of my own face.'

'I – I can tell him.'

'The gentleman, please, madam.'

'Look, here is an extra note. Thank you for your trouble.'

'No trouble, memsahib, if I can see the sahib.'

'Please go.'

'No,' said the driver with dignity, 'I am a good man, a family man, I wish to tell the sahib—'

'*Then tell me.*'

It was the Senhor's voice, the Portuguese still in his sartorial splendour ... so his appointment tonight had only been brief ... and Vasco Martinez stood while the driver assured him that he had not cheated the memsahib, that he had brought her back by the very shortest way.

'For I am an honourable man. Why should I be otherwise? Tomorrow I still have to see my fellow man's face.'

'That is so,' agreed the Senhor sympathetically. 'And for your integrity, my friend—' Whatever he put in the driver's hand silenced the driver. The man bowed, bowed to Greer, and left.

Also silenced, Greer stood waiting. Stood waiting until she could bear it no longer. Then she raised her eyes.

'It is late,' said Vasco Martinez quite expressionlessly, 'and I have had a difficult evening. We will leave it till tomorrow, Senhorita Greer.'

'Leave what?' Nervousness prompted her, but once she had asked it, she brazened it out.

'You did not think,' he said, vastly surprised, 'it finished at this?'

'Why not? As I told you before, I'm not a child.'

'Twenty and some more,' he nodded. 'The watch-girl

of Holly. But' – astonished at her thinking there was to be nothing said – 'this is my house.'

'You mean as your employee I am part of it?'

'Of course.'

'But that doesn't give you the right to question me, to direct me – I mean not in my leisure.'

'It does in my country.'

'We are not in your country.'

'How little you know, then, Senhorita Greer. *It does even more in India.*'

'Then it doesn't in Australia.'

'There was a phrase I heard in England,' he said gravely, looking her up and down, 'and it was "More's the pity". Right?'

This time she did not answer that question, instead she said, 'You – you are intolerable!'

'We will discuss that, too, in the morning.'

'Senhor Martinez, I refuse to be—'

'In the morning, *senhorita*.' He bowed for her to pass him, when she stood erect and unmoving he preceded her up the stairs himself.

CHAPTER SIX

BUT after all there was no 'in the morning'.

Greer, who had tossed throughout the night in distasteful anticipation, wished later, when the 'reckoning' she had been promised did not come, that it was behind instead of before her. At least it would have cleared the air; she hated this cloud over her head.

She had breakfasted in her room, still preferring the iced paw-paw with lime, the thin toast, the pot of Indian tea to an English sideboard offering downstairs, especially in the Senhor's company, then she had visited Holly, a very radiant Holly this morning, sitting by the window in another of her *cholis* . . . the golden lily one today . . . and a delicately patterned wrap across her knees. With her fair hair and fair colouring she looked like a flower herself. No wonder the Senhor . . . the doctor, too, for he was entering the room now, his eyes only on her sister . . . no wonder they . . . But poor Doctor Holliday, she thought at once, how can he hope to compete against a man like that? Like Vasco Martinez?

She rose unwillingly. She knew the doctor wished to check Holly, but once in the hall she herself ran the risk of encountering the master of the house, and though it would be a good thing over, that last night's misdemeanour, she did not relish that discussion he had promised.

'If you're looking for Vasco,' Terry Holliday tossed, his hand on Holly's pulse, 'he left early this morning. He'll probably be away several days.'

'Left? But . . .'

'He said something about telling you it would wait. That make sense?' He smiled at Holly. 'Young lady, you're doing fine.'

It made sense to Greer, and it also made for relief. She

went lightheartedly to the children's quarters and helped Ayah finish dressing them. She then told the nurse she would take them for their garden walk, return them when their tutor arrived to summon them to the schoolroom. Ayah bowed and beamed, and the three set off.

Somewhere in one of them, Greer thought, watching their little sandalled brown feet twinkling along the paths beneath the mango trees, should be a vein of poetry. There must be surely with a father who, while still a boy, had cried: 'The raiment Bwali wears are these . . .' There *must be*.

But— 'Get off my side of the path, you fat porpoise!' Subhas . . . or Chandra? . . . shrilled, and Chandra . . . or Subhas? . . . retorted, 'You are nothing but a bullfrog, croak, croak, croak!'

'Boys!' chided Greer in despair, not despair because of their wrangle, children would always be children, but a despair of finding that poetic vein

When one of them called 'Help, I can't swim!' and the other spoiled the ending of his joke by providing too soon 'Because you're not in the water', Greer began to think about the pool.

He, the Senhor, had been enthusiastic that the boys learn to swim, she thought, and if in his several days' absence she could teach them at least to keep afloat, achieve a few strokes, how pleased he would be. So pleased he might even forget that 'discussion'. In her enthusiasm she completely forgot the Senhor's 'Will you instruct these children *later*?' His dutiful 'That is, of course, *after* I speak with the grandparents.'

She cut short the boys' garden walk, at the same time cutting short their grumbles at being delivered to Jim before they considered they should be by telling them what she planned when lessons were over. Not such laggards today, not with swimming in view, they went into class, and Greer sought out Ayah to tell her to have their trunks ready.

Promptly at noon they descended upon her, and in five

98

minutes were splashing in the water. Greer, who had put on her own swimming things, let them play for a while, then began to instruct them.

There was little to instruct, she smiled to herself, these small boys were at the age when swimming comes as instinctively as to a little dog. Also the weather was conducive, the warm water, the pleasant surroundings. By the first lesson they could both hold themselves up.

They had another lesson in the afternoon. Greer had decided against it, not wishing to diminish their enthusiasm by making haste too quickly, but Subhas and Chandra insisted.

'Please, Miswinthrop.' They always ran the two words together. Then 'Please, memsahib.' Finally ... and how could she resist? ... 'Please, Gr-eer.' They said Greer beautifully, rolling both R's.

'Oh, all right, you ragamuffins.'

Greer had dinner that night with the doctor again.

'Soon,' he said, 'we'll be able to have Holly join us. She's coming along wonderfully. But for a while I want her to have early nights. I want her to go right back to the natural way of living, and nature intended us to sleep when it was dark.' He waved an arm towards the night outside the french windows leading to the terrace. Indian night – positive, intense, mango-scented.

'Did Vasco say anything to you?' he asked.

'Say anything to me?' Greer looked up a little alarmed. What did Terry mean? Did he know, too, about that 'discussion' that still hung over her?

'About what I would like,' said Terry Holliday. 'I mean what I would like to try out. No, I can see you don't know. Not yet. Skip it.'

The dish was *beriani*, Muslim in tradition, and a triumph of meat, rice, spices, ginger and coriander.

Afterwards Terry did not suggest sitting on the patio, and Greer was glad of that. Somehow the positiveness, the intenseness of the night disturbed her, made her restless, unsure of herself.

'The boys have worn me out,' she murmured. 'I'll go to bed.'

But before she did so, she sat at her window breathing the spicy air, for always, she had found by now, was there spiciness in the Indian air, a tang of dried herbs, smoke, fruit, jasmine petals. *And mango flowers*. That tantalizing drift now was the flower of the mango. Indian symbol of love.

The next day both boys actually crossed the width of the pool. Like everything they did, they touched the tiled rim simultaneously. For two children who were unrelated it was almost uncanny how they did everything the same. As though, Greer said to herself, they were identical twins.

But they were not. One was the child of India. One the son of Yaqub and Lalil Gupta.

Which? That was what she was here to discover. So far she had made no headway.

But she had made headway with their swimming. There would be no need any longer for watchful eyes whenever they were playing with their boats at the pool. Even if a boat foundered, its skipper would run no peril. He might only have a few dog-paddles, but that at least could keep him alive. And the way they were going they would soon have proper strokes instead of the dog-paddle. Even the Australian crawl the Senhor had spoken of.

'But what is this?'

Even as she thought of Senhor Martinez, Senhor Martinez spoke. He had come out of the house, and had Greer taken notice of his casual white suit with the collar of the white shirt left open, the white sandals, she might not have looked so apprehensively at him as she did. She might have reasoned that he had returned some time ago to be dressed in relaxed clothes like this, therefore presumably not so disapproving as he seemed.

But Greer did not think. She was suddenly remembering ... too late ... his injunctions of '*After* I speak with the grandparents' as regarded pool activities and the boys. She was realizing she had taken something on her own shoulders, and now this, as well as the reckoning she had been promised, faced her.

Looking at her and wearing, had she dared to look back, a secret amused smile, the Senhor called, 'Very well, little fishes, that's enough for a day.'

'But, Uncle Vasco, we want to show you—'

'But, sahib, watch.'

'Tomorrow. Enough now, I say. Out, Chandra! Out, Subhas!' He stood while the boys obeyed. 'Senhorita Greer, you know now where to find my study. Please to attend there in ten minutes.'

'Yes, *senhor*,' Greer said.

She saw to it that she wasn't late. But she also ... perversely ... saw to it that she was not one moment early. Whether he read the determined challenge in her attitude, she did not know. When she knocked on the door he called, 'Enter', and waved her to the seat opposite at the desk, but did not look up from his papers.

He left her stewing there for several minutes, and stewing it was, for the longer Greer waited the less challenge she found in herself. After all, she thought bleakly, all the cards are stacked on his side. I did creep out of the house that night I visited Arlene, and I was expected to wait for permission until I started the swimming instruction.

His voice cut in on her guilt, and it was so amused that Greer actually jumped in her chair.

'There, Senhorita Greer,' he said, 'is it as bad as all that, that you must trip over your bottom lip?' He paused, using the pause to take out one of his cheroots. 'Right?' he asked of his last phrase, the one with the bottom lip.

'Yes, *senhor*,' she said.

'You were naughty over the swimming lessons, yes,' he said benevolently, and the word 'naughty' made her look up incredulously at him. This formal Portuguese using such a childish admonishment!

'Ah,' he said, reading her, 'but you *are* a child, and that is why—'

'What, *senhor*?'

'I was so angry with you returning that night in a cab. Were you an experienced woman it would have been different,' he shrugged.

'No harm came,' she dared.

'It could have.' Now his banter was gone and he was looking with almost paternal sternness at her. 'But I will speak of the swim lessons first,' he said. 'You should have waited for permission, of course, but how can I be annoyed when you have already achieved so much?'

'It was not I, *senhor*, it was the boys. They're little naturals.'

'Perhaps, but you still began the process. And such an essential accomplishment, as I told the grandparents of one of them.'

'Oh, yes, *senhor*, please tell me about that.'

'They were reluctant at first, and you must see their point, Senhorita Greer, as I saw it. They had an obsession . . . right? . . . against all water. But they are intelligent, as the parents of Yaqub would have to be intelligent. They agreed that it was very important. When I returned just now to find you had decided that point yourself it was rather an anti-climax for me. Right?'

'Yes. I'm sorry.'

'You mean you are sorry for my feeling of inadequacy but not that you had already . . . disobediently . . . taught the boys?'

'Yes, I expect that is what I mean,' confessed Greer. She was looking down at the desk, but something prompted her to glance up, and to her surprise he was smiling. Smiling across at her.

'All is well,' he nodded. 'The boys can look after themselves in the water. On behalf of the grandparents of one of them, I thank you, Senhorita Greer, even if . . . oh, yes, I must slip in an admonishment . . . you acted on your own behalf.'

Greer, braver because of his praise, slipped in for herself, 'Which is strictly forbidden.'

That took away his smiling tolerance. He said, not pleased now, 'But there are *no* alleviating circumstances for your city jaunt that other night, are there?'

City jaunt . . . so that's what he thought of it! Well, let him. Far better for him to think she had been out seeing Bombay than visiting the wife of the man who had defrauded him, the man who was her uncle.

'How – how did you know I was—' she began.

'Sightseeing? The driver had told me where he had picked you up, and it was between Naoroji and Carnac Roads, so at once I knew. Everyone who comes to Bombay is anxious to visit Crawford Market. Had you waited I would have taken you myself, and by day when it is much more colourful.'

She sat silent. She had not known where she was. She was not going to tell him this, though. She would let him think what he was thinking now, and accept his censure.

It was not to be as bad as she anticipated, however. He smoked for a while, then conceded, 'Undoubtedly it has been dull.'

'What, *senhor*?'

'Your existence here. Dull, Senhorita Greer. Merely the children to occupy you, and then only at certain hours. A new city at your feet but no way to see it. Oh, yes, child, I understand. But had you come to me and said, "*Senhor*, I am bored, here is a foreign place and all I see are mango trees" I would have arranged something for you.'

'I love the mango trees,' she said. Then, unconsciously, unconscious of what he must think of her, she quoted:

'Sandals of sward, veils of the loom
Of mango (symbolled love) in bloom.'

She stopped abruptly, her cheeks flushed. She felt ridiculous.

He did not speak for quite a while, then when he did it was not to comment on the poem but to repeat . . . and kindly . . . that he understood her position.

'A young person yearns to experience a new place. Believe me, Senhorita Greer, I intended you to. But not by yourself at night. Bombay is, as I have said, no better, no worse, than all cities, but young ladies do *not* venture alone after dusk. It is very fortunate that you chose a reliable cab as you did. I must praise you at least for that.'

'Thank you.' Eyes down again.

'Tell me' . . . he paused to exhale . . . 'did the little excursion come up to your expectations? What did you see?'

Greer had a temptation to tell him that she had seen Victoria Railway Station three times, but knew that would be asking for further interrogation.

'Nothing really, *senhor*,' she blurted, 'not knowing what I was seeing.'

'There,' he said triumphantly, 'you were foolish, and you acted foolishly, but now your foolishness is forgiven. Not only forgiven, but you are assured of a *proper* tour of Bombay. Most certainly do I intend you to see it. Not only the city proper, but Bombay's countryside. You will like to visit the Aarey Milk Colony, which is set in delightful parkland. Then there are the Hanging Gardens in Nehru Park. Also, now that the little boys are fishes in water we will take them to the sandy beach of Juhu.' He was looking at her rather inquiringly. Senhor Martinez *inquiring*? But Senhor Martinez only *ordered*!

There was a slight silence, which he broke a little stiffly, no inquiry now, 'These, of course, are all only proposals.' Evidently he was annoyed at her lack of enthusiasm. She *was* enthusiastic. She *did* want to see this corner of India. If only, she thought, if only I didn't have that worry hanging over me. The worry of Arlene.

'It will be wonderful, *senhor*,' she said quickly, and he smiled that rare boyish smile of his that made him look so different.

She fidgeted, wondering what next to say, then, feeling that the interview must be at a close, went to rise.

'*Um momento*, Senhorita Greer. There is something else.' His voice was serious but not ominous, she decided. She sat back again to listen.

'Doctor Holliday has been talking with me,' he began.

'Holly—' she said urgently.

'No. No! Why do you always become alarmed over your sister?'

'Because she has always been a matter for alarm.'

'That,' said the Senhor, 'was the topic of conversation.'

'What, Senhor Martinez?'

'The doctor has come forward with a rather surprising view.'

'Yes?'

—But Greer was not to hear the view. There was the sound of sudden splashing in the pool, Ayah's voice raised in righteous indignation, running steps.

Both she and the Portuguese were in the passage together in time to see the little brown bottoms of Chandra and Subhas, who had evidently escaped from supervision to the swimming pool again, being bustled back to the bathroom. Ayah, distinctly wet, looked ready to use a brush on the receding rears, and when the Senhor said, 'And I hope she does,' Greer laughingly concurred.

'It is no use, *senhorita*,' he said ruefully, 'I cannot say what I must say here. It is a sober subject. It entails serious discussion.' For a moment he stood tapping the tips of the slim olive fingers together. 'Ah, yes,' he said at length. He looked down at her. 'You have heard of the island of Elephanta?'

'Only heard of it, *senhor*. I know it was a Hindu shrine some thousand years ago and that it's quite close to Bombay.'

'Tomorrow we will see it. And there on Elephanta,

105

away from the wrangles of small imps, we can speak. We will leave in the morning, Senhorita Greer. There is a little public launch, but I will order my own boat to stand by. You yourself must be ready around ten.'

'The children's swimming lessons?' she demurred.

'They already swim,' he pointed out. 'They now only need supervision and there is plenty of that.'

'Holly?'

'She, too, has supervision.' His eyes, the same as they always were when he spoke of her sister, were gentle. Yes, Greer thought, Holly has supervision.

'The observing I am paid to do,' she said next. – Why was she persisting like this?

He became impatient now.

'At ten in the morning, *senhorita*,' he said sharply. 'Also I am not "discussing" now, that will come later, on Elephanta. I am "ordering".'

'And you are very good at ordering, aren't you?' Only her annoyance gave Greer the courage to fling that.

A little appalled at herself, she turned and went to her room.

When she called in on Holly some time later, Greer was surprised to see Jim Matson sitting on the garden side of her windowsill talking to her.

'I thought you'd be teaching your other children on Malabar Hill,' Greer said, finding a chair.

'Actually I've been waiting for you to come down,' the boys' tutor grinned. 'I wanted to tell you that I'll take over swimming lessons tomorrow while you go out with the Senhor.'

'But how did you know I was to go with Senhor Martinez tomorrow?'

'News spreads quickly here,' Jim grinned again. 'Already I've had news of—' He glanced at Holly. 'But no, it's not for me to say, even though I'm hoping ...' He shut his lips firmly, then opened them once more to add, 'It won't be any load stopping over to give the kids a swimming hint or two, I've been longing to try out that pool and here's a legitimate excuse.'

'Thank you.' Greer did not know what else to say; she had been rather surprised at the sight of Jim perched on Holly's windowsill, she only hoped this would not be another thing disapproved of by the Portuguese. Nor by Terry Holliday, either, who now was entering the sick-room and giving looks which said unmistakably that he wanted some time with his patient.

'Well,' accepted Jim, 'up to Malabar Hill.' He jumped down from his perch, gave the girls a wave each and disappeared to the back entrance where he always parked his small car.

Greer spent the rest of the afternoon going through Holly's clothes, adding a touch here and there, a bow, a tie, a different collar, for Holly would be up quite soon, she judged, and though these frocks were simple they should be suitable for wear in the house.

She gave orders that she would dine with her sister, and since Holly herself was under doctor's orders that lights were to be out soon after the evening meal, she was back in her room again by nine o'clock. It wouldn't do her any harm to have an early night as well, she told herself, indeed it might prepare her for whatever it was that was to be discussed tomorrow.

She bathed, brushed her shoulder-length hair, then went and sat at the window to feast on the lights again, those charmingly irregular lights that became a rainbow mosaic, a kaleidoscope in greens, purples, yellows and crimsons.

There was a little crimson glow in the garden beneath her. She watched it wonderingly as it moved slowly among the trees and shrubs. A firefly? Then she smiled. The glow of a cigarette, of course. Or – a cheroot? She leaned forward slightly and breathed deeply. As well as the spice of the Indian night she caught the aroma of a cigar. The Senhor. The Senhor walking round his *palacio*, for the place was little short of a palace.

The red glow was gone now, he had moved to another

section of the garden. But still he was down there, some-where beneath the mango trees, that Indian symbol of love, and all at once Greer was feeling his presence so – so tangibly she almost felt if she reached out she would touch him.

Foolish, she tried to smile, she was a storey above the garden. But still . . . but still . . .

It was the Indian night. It was too positive, too intense. Too – disturbing. I must go to bed, go to sleep, Greer determined, be ready and calm and collected for tomorrow.

She was. In a cool cotton-knit dress she had made her-self in Sydney, sensible sandals, and, to please the Port-uguese as well as to be sensible on her head as well as her feet, the cork topee. The topee had the traditional lining of deep green, and as the cotton knit was almost an ident-ical green she felt she would not disgrace his private boat, which would be sure to be imposing, like the rest of his possessions.

But when they reached the private jetty it was not on the white and tangerine yacht the Senhor bowed her but a smaller runabout.

'It is not far,' he explained, 'even the public launch only takes some forty minutes. We are quicker and will be there in half an hour.'

He placed her among cushions, then went up to speak with his man, who had the engine ticking over and was ready to push off. Not until they had cleared the many high-powered fishing boats grouped around the rather hazy marina, hazy in the morning light, did he come back to sit beside her.

It was the usual blue enamel day. How lovely to be sure of your weather like this, thought Greer, not like Sydney with four seasons in an hour.

'Oh, we have that, too,' he smiled when she murmured this, 'only we know when to expect it by the arrival of the monsoons.'

'But it would be different again in the country,' she supposed, thinking of the tragedy that had claimed the Yaqub Gupta family, for that had *not* been anticipated.

'True, droughts and floods are unpredictable,' he sighed.

She enjoyed the leisurely six-mile run across to Elephanta, the sea so still that there was barely a ripple, and presently he drew her attention to a hilly, wooded island slowly coming into view.

'Elephanta,' he said.

The rickety little public launch that took off from the Gateway to India was in front of them, so they circled a while until the visitors got off. Then they, too, tied up at the small pier, and began the climb of two hundred and fifty feet . . . or so the Senhor said.

'But if you prefer,' he offered, 'there are porters with sedan chairs. You will find the ascent gradual, though, on long stone steps. And once on the top we can rest at an open-air café, though' . . . a smiling warning . . . 'the monkeys in the nearby trees are thieves.'

Greer found that the Elephanta caves were not really caves at all, but temples carved out of solid rock. The Senhor had engaged a private guide, and following him into the dim recesses after the brilliant sunshine was a rather eerie experience. Most of the sculptures, whispered the Senhor to Greer, depicted the Hindu god Siva. There was also a towering eighteen-foot image representing the Hindu trinity: Brahma the Creator, Siva the destroyer and Vishnu the preserver.

For all its eeriness Greer was aware of a simple grandeur, a quiet splendour. Also . . . emerging to the enamel blue again and feeling the impact of heat . . . an intenseness of feeling.

'It is difficult to believe, is it not,' asked Vasco Martinez after he had paid off the guide, 'that it is only six miles to teeming Bombay, for it is so quiet and brooding here.'

'Yes, brooding is right,' Greer nodded, looking up at

the enormous sculptures, 'but still it's peaceful and I love it.'

'I am glad of that. I come whenever I have a problem to Elephanta for that very reason. I have not a problem today but something to say. Shall we go to the café now?'

The monkeys did not thieve from their large plate of sweet spice cakes, but Greer threw them morsels. They would fall from the branches, grab the fragments and scuttle up again to regard them both once more with hopeful eyes.

'They remind me of the boys when we have a lolly scramble,' the Senhor smiled.

He was pouring more tea, fragrant, full-bodied Indian tea. Greer felt she would never drink anything else now, though Bombay, too, she had noticed, had its coffee houses.

The Senhor did not begin what he had told her he had to discuss until they were finished, and the things taken away.

'Doctor Holliday has spoken with you regarding your sister?'

'He did on the first night I was here,' Greer said, the usual alarm rising in her, the alarm that always struck when it was Holly.

The Senhor was frowning at her. 'You jump to conclusions, *senhorita*, and there is no reason for you to do so. I told you we had only come to talk.'

'I know, and I'm sorry, but always when the talk has included Holly it's been . . .' Greer bit her lip.

'Then it is not this time. It is just a "thing" of Doctor Holliday's. Can you recall what Terry spoke to you about?'

'He spoke of a lot of things. Of India. Of—'

'I meant your sister.'

'Oh, yes, I can recall,' Greer frowned slightly, remembering how she had been perplexed at the doctor's questions. What was it he had asked?

'What was actually wrong with her?' . . . 'What was her "frail" state?' . . . 'Was she protected because of that?'

She hadn't understood his trend, and now she told the Senhor so.

'You knew he was interested in psychology,' the Senhor intimated.

'He said so.'

'He feels—' The Senhor hesitated, obviously searching for words, the right words. 'He feels,' he said at last, 'that your sister may have been afforded a wrong approach to her health.'

'Wrong approach! But Doctor Jenner . . . why, he . . .'

'He was an excellent man. I do not doubt it. But he was a busy G.P., so did he have time to *study* your sister? Study assiduously? I do not wish to offend, *senhorita*, but could any general practitioner find such time?'

'He certainly was a very busy man,' Greer agreed, 'and Holly was never a straightforward case.'

'Then you see what I mean, or at least what Doctor Holliday means?'

'No,' Greer said bluntly.

'I think you are defending your good family doctor, and I applaud you for it. But I also think you are up-holding your sister's fragility, and I do not applaud you for that.'

'*Senhor!*' Greer said indignantly. When she could find words she demanded, 'Do you think Holly enjoys her ill-ness? That I enjoy it?'

'No, but I think, through the doctor, that you both have become used to it, to – well, to expect it.'

Greer looked at him dumbly. The man must be mad! One had only to look at Holly . . .

'Yes, yes.' He had read her thoughts once again. 'The child is fragile. But – *frail, senhorita?*'

'Aren't they the same?'

'There is a – nuance. That, I think, is the word.'

'It is, but – but— Oh, I only hope Holly is unaware of

111

all this, it would make her feel – well, neurotic.'

'She *is* aware of it,' the Senhor reported soberly. 'She is very keen to try out the doctor's suggestion.'

'Which is a sort of back to nature, I believe.' Greer's voice was dry.

'A trend to that direction. He wants Holly to try an uncloistered, unguarded existence for a change, see how it affects her.'

'It could kill her.'

'Not in this instance, for the doctor would be by her to watch how she proceeds.'

'I couldn't allow it.'

'But it isn't for you to say, is it?' His voice was firm yet gentle. 'She is, as you said before, a woman. She makes her own decisions.'

'She would listen to me.'

'Yes, I think she would. But would you speak to her in such a strain, Senhorita Greer, destroy a possible chance of normal living?'

'You really think that!' disbelieved Greer. 'The doctor really thinks that!'

'He would like to try it out,' Vasco said quietly, 'and there I can help him. I have this country residence. Holly could begin to find her feet there.'

'Not without me,' Greer said stoutly, then she clapped her hand apologetically over her mouth. 'That's what Doctor Holliday is out to fight, isn't it,' she said humbly, 'my smother-love. That is if a sister can have that.'

'I'm sure you never had it,' the Senhor said warmly, 'but in a way you are right. He would like Holly to stand on her own two feet. Yet not, as you anticipate, without you. He has proposed, knowing the capacity of my country residence, that we all move there for some weeks. It is an excellent place, far healthier, as it is far from city grime, than Bombay. It is rural India at its most charming. I am sure you will love it.'

'Will, senhor?'

'Holly is going. In fact I doubt if you could stop her.

Also, as the source of your employment will be transferred to there, you would not be entitled to leave my service to find another post. Even the tutor will journey to Stuyva.'

'So that's what Jim was saying ...' Greer mused aloud.

'So you see it is almost arranged,' shrugged the Senhor. 'Do not look so dubious, child, you will love my country house. It is very Indian, not at all Portuguese as here. There is much sandalwood. Much bamboo. Life is simple, uncluttered. At night you sleep on a cotton mattress on a verandah to enjoy the cool, and during the day the mattress is rolled and put away. Holly will go barelegged, often barefooted. The same golden-brown that is in your cheeks will creep into hers. There will be amusing things to do: a silkworm farm to visit, a ride on an elephant.'

'No doubt,' put in Greer accusingly, 'you have said all this to Holly?' At his calm nod she continued, 'So what can I say now?'

'Would you have said it?' he laughed, and a little breathlessly, breathless at the prospect of seeing more of India than Bombay, Greer shook her head.

It was only when he was saying in a well-satisfied voice that all was well then that Greer suddenly remembered Arlene.

'How long?' he broke in urgently.

'Time, time,' he shrugged, and gave her a reproachful look.

'How long, *senhor*?'

'You must ask the doctor, but cures are not achieved overnight.'

Nor in a week ... two weeks ... a month, Greer thought. And in that month I'll be away, and the man who is worrying Arlene, threatening publicity, will be at it again, and without my helping her, helping her to keep him appeased for a further period, the whole wretched business could break. But perhaps, her thoughts ran on, I can send her some money.

'*Senhorita*, you are not entirely in approval after all,' Vasco Martinez said in a disappointed voice.

'Put it down,' said Greer coolly, telling herself she must keep her thoughts from flickering over her face, 'that I'm not convinced.'

'But you will try it?'

'Yes.'

'Good, then.' He gave a slight sigh. 'If I have not won your enthusiasm at least I have gained your assent. I will leave it at that.'

'For how long? I mean when do you intend to move house, *senhor*?'

'When Doctor Holliday says so,' he answered. 'Perhaps some days yet.' He rose, held out his hand to assist her up, asked, 'Shall we descend?'

. . . 'Some days' at least gave her time to talk with Arlene, thought Greer, tell her she would be away. Rather relieved, she stepped ahead of the Portuguese down the first long stone step . . . and missed her footing.

She did not fall far, but she knew at once she had done something to her ankle. She drew her breath in pain as she put her foot, after he had lifted her up, to the ground.

'Ah!' he pounced.

'It is nothing. Just a wrench.'

'Perhaps, but already it swells.' He indicated the ankle that indeed was fast becoming puffy.

Ignoring her protests, he turned round and clapped for a sedan chair, its porters very eager to serve, especially since it would be a downward journey.

It did not take long to be swayed, tilted and swung to the little pier and the Senhor's boat. Not long again to be whisked back to the house on the hill.

Terry Holliday was home, and soon was examining the ankle. Nothing very much, he said, no X-ray would be necessary as the injury was quite obvious, but most certainly she would need to rest.

And who would look after her? A voice at the door

114

inquired that happily, and Holly came in. Holly! She not only came, but danced.

'My turn, Greer. Now I am the watch-girl. Whoever thought' . . . Holly almost hugged herself . . . 'I would be looking after you?'

She looked so near-radiant that Greer almost persuaded herself that this was the best thing that could have happened, an about-turn, a reversal, so to speak, Greer the patient and Holly the nurse. But only almost. With that fact that Arlene was ever-present, it could only be almost. She had to be in touch with Arlene, and confined to a couch how could she be?

The doctor must have taken her silence for pain. He promptly administered a sedative and he and Holly went quietly out.

Meanwhile Greer pondered on messengers . . . on letters . . . on the use of the telephone that was connected to every room. Surely in some way she could communicate with Uncle Randall's wife, assure her that—

Still planning, she drowsed off.

It was early evening when she wakened. Holly's little nurse was moving deftly round the room. With a nurse's intuition she sensed at once that Greer was watching her, and she put down the things she was gathering together and came across.

She smiled at Greer, but did not rearrange her pillows. 'For,' she said in explanation, taking back the hand that she had instinctively put forward, 'you are not my patient.'

'I'm not anyone's patient. I've simply a twisted ankle which already feels a lot better. Apart from that I'm fine.'

The little Indian nurse went back to the collecting of certain items round the room. She put them in a small bag.

'What are you doing?' asked Greer in surprise. 'You're not going, Elizabeth?' Many Indians, she had found, had

English names.

'Yes. I told you, I am not your nurse.'

'But you are my sister's.'

'Not any more. Now that she is your nurse how can I be nurse to her?' A little laugh. 'Please not to be worried,' Elizabeth went on, 'I think the doctor is doing a right thing letting her try herself out like this.'

'And letting her be my nurse?' disbelieved Greer. 'Holly?'

'It delights her. I think' ... seriously ... 'you always wrap her up, whereas she would like to do that to you. Do I say a wrong thing to you?' Elizabeth looked concerned.

'No, of course not. But I just can't believe it. Holly has always ... well ...' Greer looked at the nurse. 'Besides, what about you, Elizabeth? Isn't it a disappointment to leave a job like this?'

'Oh no. You see, I am' ... a moment of concentration ... 'a dedicated nurse. There is a lot of sickness here in Bombay, real sickness, and I feel I am needed more elsewhere than in this household.'

'We're going to the country. You would have liked that.'

'No, I would have felt I was not doing what I am meant to do. There is nothing more for me here. Holly can look after herself. You, with Holly's help, will soon be around again. There is no break, no sprain, only a strain. With rest and skilled bandaging—'

Greer was not listening. She was hearing Elizabeth's 'with Holly's help' and marvelling about it.

'I will leave tonight,' Elizabeth was saying. She kept on collecting her things.

A sudden idea struck Greer.

'If I wrote a letter, Elizabeth—'

'You want the writing things?' The nurse went across to the desk and brought back Holly's notepaper.

'I was wondering,' said Greer, 'if *you* could post it.'

The nurse was plainly surprised. In the big hallway the

116

household letters were always placed, and one of the servants took them away. They went to the office, Greer knew, and there they were added to the Senhor's quite considerable correspondence. The chances were the Senhor might never see a letter addressed to Uncle Randall's wife, but the chances, too, were—

So Greer took a chance on Elizabeth instead.

Remembering the symbol of love, the Indian Love Lyrics, the romance that was intrinsically in all these people ... what was it that was always said, that an Indian makes love even with his eyes! ... she sighed and murmured that it was something she had not wished to go through the usual channels.

Elizabeth was instantly enchanted. 'Ah,' she smiled, 'of course I will take and post your letter.' She quietly packed her things and tidied the room as Greer wrote, tore up, wrote again.

At length she said:

'Dear Arlene, Unfortunately I have injured my ankle and will be unable to see you for a while. But as soon as I can I will send you something, enough, perhaps, to keep things going until that person can be prevailed upon to give you a longer period of repayment. After I am better, it has been arranged that the house is closed while we all go to stay in Senhor Martinez' country residence. But please don't fear that I will desert you. I will see you before then, and will try to have something to give you, also I will make arrangements for future sums. Assuring you of my support, Greer.'

She folded and enclosed the note, thinking as Elizabeth took it with a sympathetic smile how different were the contents from what Elizabeth imagined.

Holly came in later pushing a tea wagon, a gay bubbling Holly, obviously pleased with her new role.

'Elizabeth is going,' she informed Greer, sitting beside her and eating her own dinner from a tray, the same as Greer had done when Holly was the invalid. 'She's very pleased about it. She doesn't consider us as worthy of nursing.'

'It is not that,' protested Elizabeth, very upset, for the Indians were always polite to a degree, and Greer and Holly laughed and reassured her.

'You won't forget what you promised, Elizabeth,' Holly added, and Greer gave a little start. It sounded like what *she* had been going to say, a veiled reminder about her letter, but evidently Holly had a secret, too.

'No,' said Elizabeth seriously, 'I promise you I won't.'

Doctor Holliday examined the ankle the next morning and prescribed Greer another day of having her feet up. It was pleasant enough propped by the window, listening to the children, talking to Jim who came after lessons were over. Holly, too, fluttered round all day with books and refreshments and more cushions, but not only did she render these little services, she did some serious nursing as well. This astonished Greer. Holly had never been taught usefulness. Not her fault, poor little girl, it simply had not seemed right to expect things from her.

But now she was obviously thriving on work, and it came quite forcefully to Greer that had things been better for her stepsister she would have made a wonderful nurse.

Senhor Martinez came, too, but he never stopped long. He told her that as soon as she was able to walk without feeling any weakness they would all move to Stuyva. But not before Doctor Holliday said so. 'For,' he himself said, 'a country life demands strong feet, it is not all smooth grass as it is here, there are gullies of rocks and hillsides with roots and other impedimenta.' As always, with an unaccustomed word or phrase, he raised his brow and asked, 'Right?'

'Right.'

On the second day, for the medico had decided on more immobility for Greer, the Senhor came in with a letter. He gave it to her with a smile, but Greer could barely raise a smile back. She was remembering the note that Arlene had sent her. This was in the same handwriting.

The Portuguese was unconcerned. If she had had any cause to believe he was even remotely interested in her, Greer would have put the acceptance down to the male indulgence to a female hand. But of course she had no such basis.

'Come,' he said jocularly, 'read it. Letters are sent to be read.'

'This is unimportant,' she shrugged. 'It's not from Australia, I mean.'

'Only Australian things are important, then?'

'I didn't mean that . . . I mean it's only a . . . well . . .' Now she was making something of it, the very last thing she wanted to do. 'I – I just sent for a horoscope,' she babbled, 'I saw the advertisement in the paper.'

He laughed at that and she made herself smile back.

'So already,' he told her, 'a little bit of India creeps in. By the time you have finished with Stuyva I think it will only be a small bit of Australia that is left.'

'Perhaps, *senhor*.' She glanced down at the letter.

'I believe,' he smiled again, 'for all your dismissal of its importance, you are really eager to read it. Whose horoscope are you hoping to match, Senhorita Greer?'

'What do you mean?'

'Horoscopes must match. Remember I told you that. I will leave you now, for never have I seen a more anxious face.' Again he laughed.

When he had gone Greer opened Arlene's letter. Arlene went straight to the point.

'Things are not too good, Greer. If you can help me before you go away I may be able to tide things over, but I am not sure. If possible will you come yourself. Discussions are better than writing.'

That was all she said.

That afternoon Greer tried out her foot and it felt practically as good as ever. She exercised and massaged it for hours, and the next day exhibited her progress by walking out to the breakfast room where Holly, the Senhor and the doctor were eating the morning meal.

'Complete recovery,' she showed them, and they all applauded.

'Now,' approved Doctor Holliday, 'we can move as soon as you say, Vasco.'

'I say almost at once. My business things have been attended to, and those that may occur can be looked after from Stuyva. For that matter it is only a moderate distance to return to Bombay. Those of the servants we will not need will take their holidays. The house will be closed. Will the ladies be ready to leave by tomorrow?'

Now was Greer's chance. 'There are a few things we need—' she murmured.

'Of course. I will instruct the driver to take you and Holly into the city.'

Still Greer hesitated, hating herself for what she was doing.

'And,' continued the Senhor, reading her at once, 'I will instruct my accountant to advance what will be needed for that shopping excursion. For that is what is worrying you young ladies, is it not?' he laughed indulgently.

True to his word, the accountant was waiting for Greer in the hall, and once more she went to his little office and received an advance salary. After that the girls went down the steps to the waiting car.

Luckily Holly had no head for figures. She also had simple tastes and was not really anxious for anything particular at all. 'From what I have heard,' she said dreamily, 'in Stuyva it will be a simple country life.'

'Yes, darling. Look, Holly, I've just remembered I haven't bought a pair of walking shoes for myself, a strong supporting pair, my ankle still needs help, I think. Would you be all right waiting here?' They were in a tearoom that Senhor Martinez had recommended as quiet and reliable for a mid-morning rest, and Holly nodded back happily.

'I just like sitting and watching. Don't hurry back.'

Greer wasted no time in hailing a taxi ... the house car was waiting in a parking lot ... telling the man to take the quickest route to Arlene's address. She ran up the apartment steps and Arlene opened the door. When Greer said she could not stop long the woman looked so disappointed that Greer agreed at least to have a cup of tea.

'Out here,' persuaded Arlene, 'it's cooler.' She added, 'Leave your things there.' She took Greer's arm and led her to the small verandah. 'Now tell me more about this country visit. You said everyone is going?'

'It's supposed to be a simple house, but it must be a large simple one,' laughed Greer, 'for ours is quite a large household. I expect, though, that finally it will be Holly, Doctor Terry, the tutor and myself as well as Senhor Martinez with the boys and sufficient staff to cater who will travel to Stuyva.'

'The rest?' asked Arlene sharply.

'They will take their holidays and the Bombay home will be closed. I have brought you a few notes, Arlene' ... Greer went to rise from the chair on the verandah where Arlene had placed her.

'Yes. Thank you, Greer. But just now talk to me. You don't know how lonely I get.'

It was the first time Arlene had shown any sentiment, and Greer wished she could stop longer with her. She did stop more than she had planned, but Holly, she knew, would be all right sitting in the recommended tea-room. But at last she said she must leave and she came back to where she had placed her things on Arlene's bed.

The bag was not on the bed. Then she saw she had placed it on the chair after all, not the bed. As she opened it she had an odd feeling of *not* placing it where she had found it, though, and she found herself thinking with sudden distaste of Arlene's woman-servant. She could not like the sulky, insolent girl.

However, she must be mistaken. Inside the bag everything was as it had been. The money purse that had held the notes she had received in advance still held them. Her passport. The hill house key she never used.

She gave the bundle to Arlene, Arlene arguing that she must keep some for herself.

'I have. I assure you we won't need any more.'

'You're too good. Much too good. Will you let me know when you're returning? Will you let me know if *everyone* has left the Bombay house?'

'But why, Arlene?' Greer was getting her things together.

'Because I wouldn't care to send a message there, believing you had returned, only to have it draw attention by having to be forwarded. Or, if not forwarded, more prominent than it should be by waiting in the Bombay house for your return.'

'No,' agreed Greer, 'that makes sense. You were a horoscope before.' She gave a comical shrug. 'I hardly think it would do again.'

They parted very amicably; Arlene seemed to be making a special effort. Greer was reluctantly aware that she did not really like Arlene, would never really like her, but after all, she had done no wrong, and she was genuinely trying to make amends for her husband, even though it was through his niece. In short, she was trying.

Most of all she was a relation. She belonged.

Greer peered out of the taxi to wave up to Arlene and Arlene waved back. The slats of the blind were replaced as the taxi slid round the corner.

Arlene's maid came silently forward to put something in her mistress's hand.

CHAPTER SEVEN

THE next morning, except for an essential section of the staff accompanying the party into the country, including Cook, some servants, Ayah, the accountant, and, of course, Tutor Jim, all but the gardener, who was to check the Bombay hill home occasionally, were paid up and dispatched on their annual vacations. Judging by their satisfied smiles there was a bonus with each payment.

Greer made a note on her memo as to the household arrangements. She was glad that Arlene had had the forethought to request this information. A forwarded letter, she mentally agreed with Arlene, would certainly draw attention at Stuyva; so would a letter awaiting her on her Bombay return. She did not want attention ... *Vasco's* attention ... on anything to do with her uncle's wife. She would write and tell Arlene as soon as they reached their destination.

It was a lovely departure; not such a blue enamel sky as usual, softer, gentler. The distance melted into an opalescent haze.

For a while the Senhor's car ... Holly, Doctor Terry and Greer travelled with the Portuguese, the rest in several other cars ... went with necessary slowness through the city traffic, then past the great apartment blocks.

But soon the flats were becoming more and more infrequent, the crowds beginning to dwindle. Quite soon the countryside opened up.

It proved idyllic scenery. They went through a string of little villages, the mud walls of the houses painted in whitewash and making the series seem more a long string of pearls.

Everything appeared to be white, Greer thought. There were white bullocks hauling carts, white egrets among the water hyacinth in the village ponds, Indians in spotless white *dhotis*.

Soon they began to climb, not a steep ascent, more a gentle cupping of rolling hills. In a larger village in one of these hills they had lunch . . . rice tinted with saffron and eaten with almonds.

Greer sat drinking the Indian tea afterwards, watching the women go by, like all Indian women seldom empty-handed. There would be a basket, or a water-pot, or a child. Sometimes two children.

It was a gay little town they had stopped at. The Senhor, taking out his cheroot to enjoy over his tea, said gayness was strictly a matter of districts. In another district these bright marigold and orange saris, these ochres and Spanish greens, these accompanying silver-spangled shoes instead might all be sober black.

They left the gay village to pass a series of wells; later a lake with black and white kingfishers chasing lacquer-red dragonflies.

In the mid-afternoon they came to Stuyva. It was quite small, surrounded with ripening cornfields, had a single main street lined with clumped palms with shops behind them, a string of whitewashed mud houses and a distance, once again, of gentle hills. Further back rose higher violet heights, but the Senhor said that his home was among the nearer rises.

They went down a V-shaped valley to stop fairly soon at a house that was larger, as Greer had guessed, than the simple country residence the Senhor had insinuated it was. However, from the profusion of wide verandahs, those cotton mattresses to enjoy the cool nights that he said were rolled up during the day could be true, she thought.

The girls were shown to a room, though, not a veran-dah, but at least it was Indian, not Portuguese. Stained bare floor for coolness. Bamboo instead of mahogany. Outside the window with its simple rattan blinds, rose-coloured oleanders, drumstick trees in snow-white and jacarandas in sea-blue made a flag of colour.

'And,' exclaimed Holly joyously, 'the mango tree is in bloom!'

Greer gave her a quick oblique look.

They had tea on one of the verandahs. It was hot, yet not as hot as Greer would have thought, with no coastal breeze to temper the temperature.

'We have several degrees more latitude than Bombay,' explained the Senhor, 'it makes a difference.'

After tea everyone seemed tired, even the eager boys stopped exploring and curled up into little balls on mats that were produced, and were asleep in minutes. Greer took little longer herself. One moment a clump of bee-busy bougainvillea was a crimson riot, the next only a roseate blur.

She wakened to a curious noise, and it took her a while to realize it was the trumpeting of an elephant. The friendly giant stood on the grass verge beneath their patio, tail and ears flapping. Evidently it was a household pet, and had come for its daily titbit, though titbit sounded ridiculous for a huge fellow like that.

The boys were enchanted when Vasco handed them an animal pancake to place in the big trunk. The elephant took their offerings politely and gently; when the pancake was done, trumpeting again, and when this brought no results, throwing back the trunk to open a big pink jelly cave of a mouth.

'His name is Pequeno,' Vasco told Chandra and Subhas. . . . And Greer.

The small pair laughed hilariously at that, having by now some Portuguese as well as English and, of course, their own Indian.

' "Little One" for that large elephant!' they shouted.

'Little One is also a "fond" name,' informed Vasco. He half-glanced at Greer. 'We are fond of Pequeno. Down, Pequeno.' The elephant knelt. 'Over.' Pequeno rolled out flat on one side.

'Again!' shouted the boys, but Vasco shook his head.

'One must not ask too much of a king,' he said respectfully, 'which Pequeno is, in spite of his "little" name. Shall I tell you why he is king?'

'Yes, please, Uncle Vasco.'

'It is because all the jungle is his. Among all the animals only he can push through bush that the others look at, then turn away to find an another easier track. But not King Elephant. He opens it up and passes through while the rest have to take the old beaten pad.

'Not only that, children, he can walk through grasses where you would be lost. He can blow dust or water, lift up tree-trunks. He knows all the green scents and all the whispers of leaves.'

The boys were enrapt . . . and Greer was, too.

'You should have been a father, Senhor Martinez,' she said warmly, impulsively, as carried away as Chandra and Subhas.

The Portuguese turned and smiled at her . . . but somewhere in the dark eyes the smile became an inquiry. For a moment Greer looked back in inquiry. Then she turned her glance away. He is inquiring for Holly, she knew with a hollowness that startled . . . and saddened . . . her. Inquiring of Holly's watch-girl.

She turned back to see the boys being lifted on to Pequeno's accommodating top.

'Greer, too,' they called, and the next moment she was up there as well, Vasco climbing on last of all to act the mahout.

He seemed to be practised at it, but Greer thought it would take a lot of practice for her to be a relaxed elephant rider. Although the motion was fair enough on the level grass, once Pequeno descended the gully it was like riding an earthquake.

She was glad to be off, and the boys, having accepted Vasco's ruling not to ask the king for too much at once, salaamed politely to the beast when it was over.

The rest of the household had now joined them, and Vasco showed them a little current at the bottom of the gully that ran musically into a small pool edged with flat stones.

'Senhorita Greer,' he smiled, 'will be able to continue her swimming instructions.'

'On the subject of lessons,' said Jim, coming forward, 'could you tell me, *senhor*, whether you wish the same class timetable as before?' He walked beside the Portuguese and Greer caught up with Holly.

They washed and brushed up for dinner, a leisurely meal in the bamboo room just inside the patio. After dinner they played records, read or talked. Greer said maternally once, for the habit was now imbued in her, 'Holly darling, do you think you should—'

'No.' It was Terry Holliday. Kindly but firmly. 'Leave her alone, Greer.'

'I'm sorry,' apologized Greer, 'I just thought—'

'You thought right,' laughed Holly, yawning, 'though thank you, Terry. Good night, everyone.'

Greer went with her.

'If the room becomes hot, the mattresses will be unrolled on the verandahs,' called the Senhor after them. They nodded and went out.

It was not, said Holly later in the dark, that it was so hot inside as enticing outside.

Greer had pretended not to hear for a while. She already knew what lay out there from nights in Bombay. The positiveness of an Indian evening. The intenseness. The disturbing quality.

'The moon peers, not just looks down,' continued Holly longingly. 'The stars— Oh, come on, Greer.'

They pulled on the happy coats that Greer had bought cheaply from an Eastern store in Crawford Markets, and went out.

There were figures reclining everywhere ... but there were plenty of unrolled mattresses. Holly lay down with a contented sigh, and Greer stretched out on the bed beside her. She thought of the jewel lights from her Bombay room, so different from the blackness here.

And yet not entirely black. Down in the garden a small rich glow moved backwards, forwards.

The Senhor, she thought, smoking his evening cheroot.

A shrill cacophony of birds awakened Greer. She looked around and saw that she was the last sleeper, Jumping to her feet, and drawing round her kim, she saw Holly already out in the garden and moving happily to talk to the monkeys in the banana clump. She had never seen Holly look so relaxed. She wore a short loose muu-muu, no stockings and the merest of espadrilles.

'Nature's child,' she said to herself. She thought of what Doctor Holliday had said about going back to nature. Certainly Holly had never appeared so well as now.

As she still stood there, the young doctor joined her stepsister, and at the same moment the Senhor came and joined Greer out on the verandah.

'Lazybones!' he called to Greer. Then, inquiringly as he frequently did: 'Right?'

'Right. But my sister' ... Greer waved her arm ... 'is very wide awake.' She looked at the couple by the banana clump and said impulsively, 'They make a fine pair.'

She turned away to go in and dress, but only a step away. His big arm, bare in its short-sleeved, cream silk shirt, impelled her back.

'*Um momento*.' A pause for her to obey. Then: 'You are very wrong, of course.'

'Wrong?'

'Very wrong,' he repeated. 'They are not that, *senhorita*.'

'Not what?'

'A fine *pair*.'

About to toss, 'I was only making an idle remark,' Greer flung curiously instead, 'You seem to know.'

'Oh, yes, I know.'

He still had not disengaged his hand. Adroitly Greer slipped out of his grasp and went inside.

As she pulled on a floral shift, fastened up sandals, she was aware of a stiffness inside her, an angry resentment. She had not actually meant when she had coupled Holly and Terry, she had not really intended—

But he had. The Portuguese had. And he had wasted no time in correcting her in what he had concluded in those two words of hers, that 'fine pair'. Had the correction been because – because— Now Greer was remembering the gentle looks that, from Vasco, were always *Holly*'s lot.

She felt her resentment and stiffness slowly receding. No wonder he had corrected her then. It was only natural that he should. A – man in love.

She went out to the verandah, where, by the sounds of chatter and china, breakfast was now being taken. Her resentment was gone. Her stiffness. She determined to ignore that odd little ache.

Jim conducted class under a peepul-tree, but was soon joined by a small boy in a pink tunic and baggy pants. When Krishna ... that was his name ... ran off again, Jim looked relieved, considering his own two quite enough, until Chandra blithely informed him that Krishna had gone on Chandra's invitation to fetch his 'cousin-brothers' from their houses in the valley, since they, too, might like to join in the lessons.

'Was friendliness a prominent trait in Yaqub?' Greer asked the Senhor when she came back to the house. 'And must I include any newcomers in the swimming lessons?'

He answered the latter question first. 'They will be able to swim, have no fears. As for character, you could speak with the grandparents.'

'Grandparents?' she queried.

'The parents of Yaqub. The grandparents of one of the boys.'

'But where are they?' she asked, surprised.

'Why, here, of course. In Stuyva. That is why I selected

my country residence in this district. I think I told you we used to spend vacations here with Yaqub. I grew to like Stuyva so much I chose it for my resort.'

'A Portuguese choose a resort that's not by the sea!' she taunted.

'I assure you we do not always keep to character, that is the character that has been internationally assumed for us.'

'Was seafaring only ever assumed, then?' She did not know why she was parrying with him like this.

'You know it was not,' he said reproachfully, 'you know we had knowledge of the seven seas when you were barely leaving your harbours.'

'Oh, yes. Except that your namesake didn't venture south, Australia would be— Well, what would it be, *senhor*?'

He shrugged in annoyance. 'You are in a difficult mood. I am just trying to tell you that when it comes to facets in character . . . right?'

'Right.'

'We have as many as the British. For instance our formality is always taken for granted.'

'But aren't you formal?'

He ignored her. 'Also, as a race, although proud of our dark beauties, we are reputed to find a dangerous softness in us to the fair Anglo-Saxon type.'

Emphasis on the fair, Greer thought. She said impertinently, not knowing why she did, 'And do you?'

His face had darkened at her bantering tone. 'Yes, *senhorita*,' he said deliberately, 'indeed I do.' He looked hard at Greer's dark brown, not pale, hair.

The cousin-brothers of Krishna's did not turn up after all, nor did Krishna, so the small swimming pool was not overcrowded. It proved a delicious place, gaining in the musical tinkle of its cascading water what the turquoise pool gained in its gleaming tiles and modern touches.

Refreshed, they came back to the house, then, the meal over, the Senhor told Greer that he was driving the boys across to see the grandparents of one of them, and that he wished her to come.

She did not obey with much alacrity. Her initial feeling of repulsion at the post he had asked her to take on, that anger she had known that first day in his office because of the 'observations' she would be expected to make, came flooding back again. Once more she knew she liked nothing about this business, this child selection as it were. All children, she thought again, *all children* were love.

It made it much worse, she thought next, that the small boys, seated in the back of the car, were quite happy about it all. They spoke cheerfully between themselves of 'Your grandfather, perhaps' . . . 'My grandmother as she may be.'

'It's wrong,' Greer said softly to herself.

'It does not fret them,' the Senhor, who heard her in spite of the softness, shrugged.

'They should never have learned of the situation.'

'That is regrettable,' he admitted, 'but the tragedy received much publicity, and sooner or later they would have known. Much better for them, it was decided, to have grown up with the story than to be acquainted with it when they were adults.'

There were several houses like the Senhor's tucked in the dents of the hills, Greer noticed, and he told her that Stuyva was considered a favourable district for relaxation.

'It is healthy, and older couples often retire here. Younger couples make it a second or holiday home.'

He drew her attention to the architecture. 'These houses,' he said, 'are bungalows. Originally they were erected in Bengal and known as Bengal houses. It diminished to bungalows, and Europe . . . Australia, too . . . copied the name.'

Greer quite liked the simple structures, mostly a central room around the outside of which was a continuation of verandah covered by an extension of the roof.

The Gupta house when they reached it was a similar

style, only much larger and more elegant, many arches and lattices had been added, screens and frescoes. It was painted white.

The Guptas came out to greet them, and Greer noticed that their embracing of the two boys was strictly equal.

Tea was served in the little courtyard where there was actually a peacock, and this entertained the boys while the older ones talked. The Guptas spoke at once of Greer's curious assignment. They were extremely intelligent, and assured her that they very much regretted the knowledge the boys had of the affair.

'But it was very publicized,' sighed Mr. Gupta, saying what Vasco had said. 'What else could we do? Also, children usually accept a fact, whereas—'

Greer, sorry for their distress, discarded her previous attitude and said warmly, 'It doesn't worry them, they're both very outgoing little boys.'

'Yes,' said Mrs. Gupta, puzzled, 'which Yaqub was *not*. He was a dreamer. Withdrawn, really.' She got up and came back with some books. They were their only son's compositions. Greer read them through, impressed by the feeling and the fluency.

'We love both these children,' Mrs. Gupta said. 'Whichever is our son's son, it will make no difference to our love. But we would' . . . she touched the books . . . 'like to give these to Yaqub's own son.'

'Of course,' Greer said softly; she felt different about it all.

The peacock was putting up its tail, but instead of being inspired by the colours, the boys were arguing how long it could keep it up.

'It is possible,' Greer said thoughtfully, 'that mechanics will appeal more to *both* of them.'

'We realize that,' they nodded. 'A gift or talent does not necessarily have to be handed on.' But the eyes of both the older people went wistfully to the volumes in Greer's hand, and she knew what they were feeling.

On an impulse Greer said sincerely, 'I *do* understand,

and I will try to help you. I admit I did not agree with your wish at first, but when I read your son's poem "Bwali"—'

'Ah, yes, "Bwali",' nodded Mrs. Gupta. 'How he loved Bwali.'

'The words were very beautiful,' Greer assured her.

'As it is beautiful, even though it is not a shrine any more like Madura's, like— But of course' ... nodding at Greer ... 'you will see it.'

'I would like to some time.'

'While you are here,' Mr. Gupta assured her. 'At Stuyva. It is only a very moderate distance.'

'Bwali is?' Greer felt an odd pounding in her heart. All at once she was a schoolgirl again, and turning over the pages of a travel book, and there it was: The Pool of the Pink Lilies.

She raised her eyes and met the eyes of the Senhor. For a moment their glances merged.

'But it is not the lily time yet,' Mrs. Gupta was saying. 'Yet soon, would you say?' She looked at her husband.

His reply was drowned in the boys' shrill laughter as they chased each other to tickle the other with a feather the peacock had discarded. It was an opalescent feather of royal blue and green, a really beautiful thing. Greer wondered if Yaqub would have used the feather for this tickling purpose, and smilingly said so.

The grandparents said yes ... but he would have written a poem as well.

They were delightful people, and Greer was glad Vasco had taken her to meet them. Now she felt quite assured that if a solution happened, if it ever could happen, it would make no possible difference.

Going back in the car the Senhor said, 'You are satisfied?'

'Yes. Mrs. Gupta told me that if they learned a fact, it would not even be made known to anyone. Only the books and poems would be willed later on.'

'That is true, but I don't think they can learn,' he said.

'No,' she agreed .. but she was thinking suddenly of Bwali, Bwali to which the father of one of them had spilled words from his young eager heart.

Bwali! The odd excitement throbbed up in her again, yet not odd really, for in all the years since she had read that travel book, she had remembered, remembered vividly, turning that page.

She was going to take the boys to the shrine, she knew. Take them and observe them. The Pool of the Pink Lilies. She half-closed her eyes in a delight she did not really understand; could only sense.

The cool fingers of the Senhor aroused her. They had come back to the house and he was helping her from the car. She knew she should tell him her plans, for that was what she was here for, to help him in this observation, but stubbornly she determined not to. She did not even look at him as she stepped out, though she knew he was looking at her.

She went into the house . . . to Holly sitting on a chair and the doctor sitting on the chair's arm, his arm intentionally around her.

Now Greer *did* look at the Senhor, and her glance flicked remindingly at him.

'You are very wrong, of course,' he had said, 'they are not that. Not a fine *pair*.'

She smiled coolly, meaningly, but receiving no acknowledgment, she turned and went to her room.

She did not sleep much that night. The knowledge that somewhere quite near her lay the Pool of the Pink Lilies, that first girl dream, and that dream ever since, kept coming back to her. She longed to ask Where? How one got there? But the person who would know most of all was the one she could not bring herself to approach. She could not ask Vasco Martinez and she could not have said why.

It was not a punishment not to sleep here in Stuyva, she thought, staring into the tropical darkness. The moon was a golden flower, the stars bigger than she had ever seen before. Birds, too, entertained at night as well as day . . . jars, owls, the curious-noted brain-fever birds.

So warmly relaxed was the air, so inviting, that she got silently up, pulled round the happy coat, and went and perched on the verandah rail.

She could hear the squirrels foraging . . . or perhaps it was monkeys. She blinked a few times to sharpen her night vision.

After a while she glimpsed a bright black eye and a floating tail, so knew it was a squirrel, for the monkeys either curled or extended their tails, not used them in graceful floating movement like this. She watched the flicking and floating as the little creature rummaged for seeds or berries, holding the find delicately in its hand to eat it at once, its bright eyes darting watchfully as it did so.

One of those quick darts focused Greer and at once the Indian squirrel froze where he perched, pretending by his stillness not to be there.

Greer was fascinated . . . she saw the berry still held aloft but the paw not moving. She could not refrain from letting out a soft giggle.

A very unusual thing happened . . . or so Vasco told her soon afterwards.

The squirrel fell. Personally, the Senhor said later, he had not seen one fall before, but watching Greer watching him, the squirrel must have lost his balance. Greer was upset. The little fellow appeared to fall quite hard. She jumped down over the rail and ran to pick him up, but a voice came out of the darkness, a quiet but firm voice: 'No, not that way. This way.' It was Vasco Martinez. With an experienced hand he was picking up the little thing. 'They have long sharp teeth,' he explained, 'they can inflict a wound. Scared and hurt like this, it is likely he will turn and dig in those rodent teeth.'

'How hurt?' asked Greer, distressed. The squirrel had been such a bright-eyed little fellow.

'By rights he shouldn't be hurt at all, squirrels should

fall quite lightly, they can if they try, but this fellow's fall took him completely by surprise, and it will be the shock, not the injury. Can you fix up a soft bed for him to curl up on?'

'Of course.' She was hurrying into the bungalow finding a box and a cushion. Behind her came the Senhor, bearing the inert squirrel. He seemed to be experienced in animal-carrying, and Greer said this.

'Yes, Terry, Yaqub and I doctored many animals when we stayed at Stuyva, though not, as I said, a tumbled squirrel. I think Terry first got his doctoring urge from attending these small emergencies. Though it was Yaqub who had the bush knowledge. For instance from Yaqub we learned that death comes for animals as it does for humans, and that is mainly in the night-time. If you can sit with them, even if you are not a friend, even if they do not understand you, often they will recover.'

'Then let me,' said Greer quickly, and he smiled back at her, but a completely different smile now, no banter in it, no innuendo. Just two people anxious over a squirrel.

'We will *both* sit, Senhorita Greer. You do not mind missing your sleep, then?' He had brought across a cushion and put it down for her on the floor. He sat down himself.

'It is no hardship, *senhor*,' she said. 'Indian nights are – they are—' She could not find a word.

'Yes,' he agreed. 'But' ... looking at her closely ... 'was it only the beauty of the night that kept you awake this night?'

It was not, and Greer had a suspicion that he knew as well as she knew, she remembered how their eyes had met and merged when Mr. Gupta had said: 'While you are here you must see Bwali.'

But for the same inexplicable reason as before, Bwali, between them, between her and the Senhor, could not be spoken.

'The nightjars awakened me,' she evaded. 'And then

that other bird.'

'The brain-fever,' he nodded. He bent over the little squirrel. 'I do not think it is badly hurt, but even without an injury, if we left it alone probably in the morning it would be dead. Need is a powerful thing, you agree, *senhorita*?'

She said, 'Yes, *senhor*,' in a low voice.

'And this squirrel has need of us. Undoubtedly if he recovers he will turn and hurry away from us, and without a backward glance, but now . . .' He gave a little shrug.

Several times in that night vigil his hand went to his pocket for his cheroots, then he remembered their sick ward and with a gesture of contrition he withdrew his hand.

Once he got quietly up and brewed some coffee.

In between he spoke about India, told her things that left her waiting, breathlessly, for more and more . . . the walled city of Orchha . . . the impact of the Taj Mahal . . . the Pearl Mosque of Aurengzeb where the Great Mogul had had inscribed: 'If there is a paradise on earth, it is here, it is here.'

The little squirrel gave a deep breath and the Senhor said, 'I believe he's snoring.'

They laughed softly together.

'It is here, it is here,' Greer repeated dreamily. She liked the sound of the words.

'They are written in Delhi,' explained Vasco, 'but I think there could be paradise much nearer Stuyva.' He was looking at her obliquely again.

Hurriedly Greer said, 'Yes, I must see Stuyva. We went through so quickly.' She knew, though, that it was not Stuyva that Vasco had been talking about.

'Yes, do so,' he invited. 'There is a goldsmith's shop that will interest you.'

'A goldsmith? In a small place like this?'

'In India even if people are shabby they still must have jewels. Besides being an investment they have a love for them just for their beauty. Yes, you must go into Stuyva and inspect their ankle chains, necklaces, ear, finger, toe-rings. They will delight you.'

'Only gold?'

'Silver as well. Precious and semi-precious stones.' He paused a moment. 'Do you drive, Senhorita Greer?'

'Yes.'

'Then I will lend you one of the small cars I have here. You may care to drive your sister around at times while the boys are at lessons. Already the tutor has a car, and he is planning outdoor studies for his pupils. Perhaps, too, you will occasionally go along with them. Children are often revealing in their attitude to nature.'

'Yes, I will, *senhor*, but the one car surely would do, I mean we could all use it.'

'Not in this little model,' he smiled, 'and certainly you would never want Chandra and Subhas in the gold-smith's. It would be like' . . . he thought a moment . . . 'a bull among pottery. Right?'

'We say in a china shop. But' . . . a smile . . . 'I see your point. Thank you, *senhor*. A car would be nice.' Because she knew that, being the Senhor, he would be thinking of *one* journey in particular she was planning, she found she could not look up at him. Hastily, so hastily it must have shown, she started on another trend.

At the first buttering of dawn a curious thing happened. The squirrel, without any preliminary trying out of injured limbs, simply stretched, then streaked from his bed on to the verandah. From the verandah to the nearest tree. The bounding, flowing movement was so quick that one moment they had a squirrel, the next an empty box.

'I told you,' said Vasco. 'They are ungrateful children.'

'But alive,' Greer rejoiced. She yawned and tried out her cramped limbs. The verandah sleepers were waking up, so it was no use thinking of catching up on lost hours.

Anyway, the bright daylight would soon see to that.

Refreshed by coffee, Greer took a walk with the boys,

then when they were claimed by Jim she spent some time in the class with them.

'Senhor Martinez tells me you, too, have a car at your disposal,' Jim said as the boys worked on a composition. 'I was afraid of that.' At her look of inquiry he grinned, 'They are *very* mini cars. There has to be an extremely close settlement.'

She smiled back, remembering how he often sought out Holly. 'Too bad, Jim,' she sympathized.

'Two cars will be handy, though,' he went on, 'especially as the Senhor and Terry will be away in the big one for the next few days. We could never fit the three adults and the two imps into one Mini.'

'So they're leaving us,' Greer mused.

'Yes, some estate or other that Senhor Martinez is interested in buying. Our doctor is going to look over the health angle. Show me what you have written, Chandra, if you don't intend to write any more.'

Greer rose. Jim's demand to see Chandra's writing had reminded her that *she* had some writing to do. To Arlene. Now was her chance when she could see to the posting of the letter herself. She and Holly could send it away when they drove into the village.

The Senhor sought her out soon afterwards to show her the car, a small manoeuvrable one which should cause her no difficulty used on the established roads.

'I would not take the car on any track, though, Senhorita Greer.'

'No, *senhor*.'

He stood looking at her a moment as though to ask her something, then he must have changed his mind.

'I will be absent for the rest of the day, probably tomorrow, the day after.'

'Yes, the boys' tutor told me.'

'You will remember not to venture too far at this juncture.' Again the long look.

Greer was thinking only of the letter. 'All we will do,' she assured him, 'will be to go into the town.'

He went soon afterwards, and almost at once his accountant sought Greer out. 'The Senhor wishes me to advance you this sum.'

'But this is not right; I was paid last week.'

'Nonetheless,' smiled the man, 'he says that a goldsmith's shop is a fascinating place.'

'He is very good,' said Greer. She was thinking with relief that she could send the money to Arlene.

After lunch, the two girls got into the small model and took the winding road into Stuyva.

There was none of the bazaar spirit of the Bombay markets, they found, but the shops selling spice and herbs were there, the copper pot shop, the trays of strung jasmine. And the goldsmith's.

Holly looked wistfully at the goldsmith's wares, and Greer had an impulse to take the notes out of the envelope marked for Arlene and buy her sister that filigree necklace that she held lovingly in her thin hands instead.

But she knew that Holly would understand the position and agree to what she was doing, and except that she did not want her involved, Greer would have confided in her at once.

Instead they had coffee at a coffee house, Greer taking out her little memo book to check Arlene's address.

Holly suddenly called for her attention. There was a small procession passing along the street.

'He must be a Mogul at least,' she said of the young man's finery.

The coffee proprietor explained in his honeyed English that he was a bridegroom. Grooms wore the costume and stage jewellery of a rajah, he recounted.

They enjoyed the little tableau, the hired elephant with its ornaments and draperies of scarlet and gold, the resplendent groom, the beautiful bride, the many attendants. They returned reluctantly to their coffee when the procession was over, but discussed it at length with their host. Then Greer addressed her letter and they posted it.

As they left in the car for the house in the hills again, the coffee man ran out of his shop with a small leather book in his hand.

'Memsahibs,' he called, 'memsahibs!' But they were chattering about the wedding again and did not look back.

He shrugged and put it aside with its addresses and its notes. One of the notes Greer's reminder to tell Arlene that during their absence in the country only the gardener would be in attendance ... occasionally ... at the Senhor's Bombay house.

CHAPTER EIGHT

GREER did not miss her memo book. She had no occasion to consult it, so she did not discover its absence. The next few days were spent busily, enjoyably, and ... or so Greer considered ... gainfully. For Greer felt at last that she made a forward step in her observation of the boys. Though this satisfaction did not come until nearly the end of the Senhor's and the doctor's absence.

But previous to that, the hours fairly flew. There were many interesting things to see in Stuyva, intriguing things to do, and with a car at one's disposal, apart from the several hours spent with Chandra and Subhas, in Holly's case hours spent with Jim Matson, the girls were never home.

Often Greer thought about those hours that Holly spent with the young teacher. Holly previously the little recluse, recluse because of her delicate health, now adding Jim Matson to these new strings to her bow! There could be no jealousy in Greer when it came to Holly, Holly had been deprived of so much she could only feel pleasure in her stepsister's pleasure, but there could be, and there was, a note of warning. The same warning she had received in Terry Holliday's interest in Holly. It was the sound of the Senhor Martinez's displeasure. For *he* was interested in Holly, too. He had shown it clearly Expressed it clearly. And the Senhor was the one who counted.

Greer now measured the times the two, Holly and Jim, paired off together, and felt an unease. Yet her good sense told her that it was only natural that two young people should seek each other when they were off duty ... not duty for Holly, she had no duty save the duty of regaining her strength ... but duty for Jim. It was only natural that they took the advantage of Greer's supervision of the boys to enjoy each other's company.

Assuring herself of the usualness of it, Greer now took the hands of Chandra and Subhas, and once more, in the pool at the bottom of the garden, or on a walk, endeavoured to 'observe'. The trouble was, she thought ruefully, the two children did things almost uncannily together, making it near impossible to 'observe'.

Trying to make her see something in a tree that they could see but she couldn't, they directed severely and in precise unison: 'Greer, lòok where we're putting our eyes.'

She laughed at the phrasing, but not at the instinctive unison We. Our. Us. How could she report anything to the Guptas when these two boys even *saw* the same things? But she did not think about it then so much as later. And then she *did* think.

Meanwhile the car excursions proved delightful. Motoring in India, Greer had previously found, once off the more controlled motorways could be a very slow business, not because the roads were bad but because of the animals that inhabited them. The ways now of Stuyva proved just as frustrating if charming. Bullocks harnessed to carts had to be given right of way, goats driven by goatherds in search of new pastures. Once they even encountered a lazy water buffalo who evidently preferred the dusty road to his own background. He looked back at them with his china-blue eyes, no doubt aware of his rights, for with the exception of wild game, most animals led a sacred life in this India.

There were also crows, doves and innumerable tree squirrels to impede progress, for the roads were always tree-lined, generally the ficus family, and the creatures came after the hard little figs.

On one of these interrupted journeys, Greer, as she waited for a clear path, mentioned to her stepsister ... casually, she hoped ... the many times that Holly and Jim appeared to seek each other's company.

'Yes.' Holly actually gave a little shiver of joy. 'Oh, *yes*, Greer.'

143

Her agreement startled Greer, but she hoped she did not show it. However she could not refrain from a spontaneous 'But, darling—' ... Holly, she really wanted to remind her, there has also been the doctor, and although I know you don't mean anything, although I know that all this is new and sweet and very flattering to you, you ... well, you just can't, Holly. You *can't*. Especially – particularly where there is also – the Senhor. At that 'Senhor' Greer knew a sharp pain in her that she had known once before; it had been that morning when Vasco had denied that Holly and Terry made a fine *pair*. She tried to thrust the ache aside, but it was no use, it persisted. I mustn't permit it, she knew. I mustn't feel like this.

She became aware of Holly's inquiring eyes on her, inquiring what she had to say.

'Darling,' she said inadequately, 'you and Jim ...'

'Oh, yes, you must wonder,' trilled Holly joyously, 'and I wish I could tell you, but I can't, Greer, not yet, not until ...' Another happy shiver.

'But Doctor Terry—' Greer said inadequately as before. Surely even an inexperienced girl must know that she couldn't play around like this.

'Yes, Terry's in the picture, too,' Holly admitted quite calmly.

'Holly!' A pause. Then: 'That only leaves the Senhor.'

'But he is the important one,' Holly announced. She mused a moment. 'Without Vasco it just couldn't come true.'

Greer put her foot on the clutch, got into gear, released the brake. She startled some tree squirrels and nearly knocked over a cow.

'There's a temple we haven't visited yet,' she said a little faintly. She did not know about Holly, but she would have traded all the carvings, paintings, miniatures ... and that pervasive smell that went with these aged interiors ... for one honest interchange with her stepsister. But how could she ask Holly? Eager-for-life little

Holly? Holly of whom Doctor Jenner had quietly said '. . . why not?' '. . . may as well'. . . 'Let her go.'

So they set off for the little mosque Greer had been told about, awaking the guardian who was taking his siesta on a grass mat at the bottom of the steep steps.

They also explored ruins with vermilion pomegranate flowers growing out of tumbled walls. They visited old gardens with fountains that played no longer, only gently broke the looking-glass surface of the pools.

But Greer would not go to the Pool of the Pink Lilies.

'You always wanted to see it,' Holly reminded her once of the old Shrine.

'It's down a narrow track. I said I would keep to the roads.' That could not sound convincing, Greer knew, not on a narrow road like they were traversing now, but Holly did not argue.

She did say, though, that it might have been interesting to have observed the boys there.

Greer answered non-committally and changed the subject, but evidently Holly kept it in view, for the next afternoon not only she and Jim went off together, they took Chandra and Subhas with them.

Greer heard all about it over tea later.

'The lilies are not out yet,' Holly told her. She must have sensed a wish in her stepsister not to be told more about the shrine, for she touched next on the boys.

'It did nothing to them, Greer,' she reported. She glanced at Jim for his opinion.

'Nothing,' he nodded. 'No feeling at all . . . except a disgust that there was nary a tadpole,' he laughed.

'No doubt a mutual disgust?' queried Greer.

'Isn't everything mutual there?' Jim shrugged. He looked across at Holly and raised his brows in inquiry. She nodded back to him, got up and the pair went off together.

After a while Greer sought out Chandra and Subhas.

She watched them as they tried to dam up the creek with stones and pebbles; they were very methodical youngsters, she thought, very much on the practical side. Still, a poet could be methodical, practical, too; just because words sang in him it did not mean he had nothing he could do with his hands.

She smiled at the little figures plodding backwards and forwards. One of these small people was the son of a man who had been one of three close friends. Part of a trinity. One of them also was the Senhor's godchild. She tried for a moment to get a feeling out of that, but it was no use. The two, she thought, could have been the one boy.

She took them across to the Guptas again, recounting to the older people what Jim had recounted of Bwali.

'Oh, yes,' they nodded, 'that was also done earlier by Vasco. The boys were not at all impressed, he said. But after all, is any child?'

'Yaqub's child?' asked Greer gently.

Greer asked them next about the mother, the wife of their son, why hadn't her parents tried to help? But Lalil's parents had died soon after her marriage, they told her, they had never seen their grandchild.

'There is no one left on her side,' they sighed.

Where she had been reluctant before, now suddenly Greer found herself eager ... anxious ... to help. She studied the children continually. She asked searching questions of the Guptas, sensitively at first, then, when she saw that time had softened the sharpness of their loss, with more directness. She asked where the unfortunate village had been.

'As the crow flies,' said Mr. Gupta, 'it was not far away.' He led Greer to the window and pointed to a distant hill, one of those violet rises behind the gentler slopes. 'The fated small place where Yaqub was performing his work was on the other side of that taller peak,' he said.

'But that's almost close,' mused Greer. 'Could I go there?'

'From here, from Stuyva, only this route.' Mr. Gupta produced a map and demonstrated a track that entailed many more miles than the crow would need. 'There is a shorter road from the motorway,' he added. As she studied the legend he explained, 'The flood came down here.' He pointed. 'Taking all before it.'

'All except—'

'Yes, all except those two children, and one of them ...' He made a little gesture.

But Greer was thinking in a different strain. 'All except two children.' But had there been ... could there have been ... a third?

'I'd still like to go,' she said quietly.

'There is nothing there,' he told her just as quietly. 'The village has never been rebuilt.'

'But I'll see it all the same.'

The Indian smiled tolerantly at her. 'That was done, of course, but there was nothing. Nothing. Only the two children remain of that sad place.'

Also a third child? Greer's mind returned to that again and again. The thought reared up once more in an episode that occurred just before the Senhor's return.

Like all children the world over the two Indian boys were more demons than angels, and the trick was to keep them occupied so that mischief was kept at bay. There was much to be said, said Jim, for that time-honoured theory on idle hands.

So when Jim was not teaching, Greer was diverting, but inevitably two little boys had to find themselves alone. Within a remarkably short space of time they created a situation that probably had been created many times before all over the world, but it was the thought that the occurrence evoked that struck Greer so forcibly.

Chandra ... or was it Subhas, for she still had difficulty with their identities, and so did Jim ... decided to discover how the water went down the sink, and in doing so entrapped three of his small brown fingers. Being a resourceful child, or perhaps anticipating a scolding, he did not call out for quite a while, but tried to free himself. Then he pulled the fingers the wrong way, and pain pushed aside resource and caution, and Chandra . . . or Subhas? . . . yelled. As a matter of fact both children yelled, but Greer did not consider this until later.

The cries soon brought the household, with Jim, Holly and Greer to the distressed boy, and for an hour they worked on the trapped hand. But the bruised fingers had swollen considerably and now the entire palm was over the drain-hole.

Jim, lying on his back on the floor to consider the scene, said there was nothing else for it than to cut away the grill with a hacksaw blade. 'But it will have to be done carefully, and the fingers guarded, otherwise we could cut them off.'

'Get me out!' cried Chandra in Indian, English and Portuguese. Subhas cried out exactly the same words in the same languages in the same routine, but in the anxiety of the moment it was not noticed.

The hacksaw was produced and the men took it in turn to cut at the grill, Greer nursing the little boy in comforting arms. Once the child accidentally grabbed at the tap with the free hand and sent a flood of water on Jim and while he dried off someone else took over, still carefully shielding the trapped, bruised, badly swollen fingers.

It seemed an eternity before they had him free, and all the time the two boys cried together, stopped together, began again.

Once, towards the end of the ordeal, Greer glanced across at the free child and saw that the little boy was holding his hand in exactly the same prisoned position as the trapped boy. His face was twisted with fear and pain like the other little face. And when at last freedom came both boys had swollen hands. *Both* boys.

Greer simply stood looking down on the two pairs of red, burning, throbbing fingers. It couldn't be! She had read of such things, of course, in identical brothers, but

Chandra and Subhas were not. Yet throughout the ordeal they had wept at the same time, been soothed together—

What was this?

And those were Senhor Martinez's opening words a few minutes afterwards. In the heat of the episode no one had heard the returning car, they had not seen the doctor and the Portuguese enter the bungalow.

'What's this?' Vasco Martinez called from the door.

It was odd, Greer thought afterwards, how with the arrival of the Senhor everything seemed to become calm again. The children's cries diminished, the episode became a minor domestic happening, the flood of water on Jim even a humorous interlude. And the swelling went down on the bruised fingers. Greer did not look at the fingers of the child who had not undergone the ordeal. I imagined they were sore and red, she said to herself ... but she knew she could not put down to imagination that joint suffering, those chorused cries.

The children were comforted by a small stray black lamb that the Senhor and Terry had picked up on the road and brought home to them. The nightmare forgotten ... 'How could it be a nightmare, Greer, in the day, why isn't it daymare?' they demanded ... they bore Mr. Black as they named him down the gully to be taught to swim.

'Only not too much at once, darlings,' Greer pleaded, 'he's not like a dog who loves to splash.'

Not satisfied that they heeded her, and feeling sorry for the little black stranger, Greer quickly swallowed the tea that had come in, and started off to follow the boys down. She became aware that Vasco Martinez was accompanying her.

'Do not worry, Senhorita Greer,' he told her, 'already they love Mr. Black and will see he comes to no harm.'

'Yes, I suppose you're right, but he is a bereft small creature.'

'Only Mr. Black?' He looked down at her quizzically.

'It seems there are other bereft little creatures,' he said gently.

She flushed, knowing he was speaking of her troubled countenance. She had got over her relief at Chandra's . . . or Subhas's? . . . freedom now, and was pondering again on the boys themselves. Yet she had been as bright as the rest of the tea-drinkers just now, she thought, so how had he noticed her preoccupation?

'Oh, yes,' he nodded, 'I saw that you had other thoughts of your own. Can you tell me, Senhorita Greer?'

'I must,' she answered. 'It is, of course, the boys.'

'Of course?' He picked her up a little sharply. 'Must all your thoughts always be for the children?'

'That's what I'm here for, *senhor*,' she reminded him.

'Not entirely, *senhorita*.'

She thought a moment about that, then nodded. 'I understand – Holly.'

He did not comment. He walked in silence a few minutes. Then he demanded rather sharply, 'Those thoughts, *senhorita*?'

'I feel at last I have come a step forward in the observation you required of me.'

'Yes?' He was all interest now, his coolness gone. 'And which of the children—'

'Neither, *senhor*. I mean—'

'Yes, *senhorita*, what do you mean?'

'The wonder has been building up for some time. I mean to say it just didn't occur now.'

'With the finger business, you mean?'

'The finger business,' she nodded. 'But that was the climax.'

'Of what?'

'Of a feeling that Chandra and Subhas are – brothers. Oh, they must be, *senhor*, otherwise—'

'Otherwise?'

She recounted her impressions in an eager, rather breathless voice.

150

'They think the same. They act and they react the same. They see the same things, express them similarly. They . . . oh, Senhor Martinez, they even both *suffered* together just now.'

'Surely not such an unusual thing when two children have been reared together,' he pointed out reasonably.

'Both held their little hands in pain. I truly believe both felt the pain. And I feel, *senhor*—'

'No,' he interrupted, 'that has all been looked into.' He stopped, stopping her with him, and took out, clipped and lit a cheroot.

'It has been looked into, child,' he said kindly, 'naturally, no rock has not been uncovered . . . right?'

'No stone has been unturned,' she said mechanically, 'but—'

'This unhappy village had no children in it at the time except the child of Yaqub and his wife Lalil and a small boy companion of the same age as the son. There was an experiment going on in this village, and that is why at the time of the disaster there was not the normal population. So you see if two little boys escaped they *must* have been those two and no others.'

'Yes.' But Greer said it unwillingly, still unconvinced.

'*Senhor*,' she said presently, 'I would like to see the valley. I know where it is.' She turned towards the distant rise that Mr. Gupta had pointed out. 'I know also that the road from Stuyva to it is a long winding one, but—'

'It is already done, *senhorita*,' he promised, 'we will leave tomorrow. Early, of course, for it is as Mr. Gupta said a long way.'

'Thank you, *senhor*.'

They walked in silence for a while, then Vasco told her, as Mr. Gupta had told her, that she would find nothing there.

'I myself have taken the boys,' he added, 'so it would be of no use repeating that experiment.'

She smiled at that disclosure, telling him about Jim's

151

and Holly's experience at the Pool of the Pink Lilies.

'There was no soulful reaction,' she related wryly, 'only a disgust at the absence of tadpoles.'

'You report to me what they reported,' the Senhor said a little sharply, 'what the tutor and your sister reported. Do I take it then you did not visit that place yourself?'

Greer in her turn took the sharpness in his voice as a criticism, and she said humbly, 'No, I didn't go. I'm sorry, *senhor*.'

'Why did you not go?'

'I – I—' But she could not find the words. She barely knew herself why she hadn't gone. She mumbled something about Mrs. Gupta saying the lilies were not yet out, but she knew it was not that, it was something that had to be kept until – until—

She stopped momentarily on the track, recovered herself and began walking again. Normally, she hoped.

For the thought . . . no, the *knowledge* in Greer in that moment was that the Pool of the Pink Lilies had to be kept for – him. For Vasco Martinez. Which meant, she knew foolishly, knew emptily but knew surely that she would never see it, because Vasco had no interest in it, no interest in it . . . *with her*.

They had reached the creek now, and they sat on a rock and smiled at the children gambolling in the crystal shallows. The little black lamb was lapping contentedly from a small dam the boys had enclosed in a little circle of stones.

While they were there the mahout brought Pequeno down for his daily dip, performed in a pool below the children's, and just as well, for Pequeno enjoyed every moment of his splash, and left the pool in an extremely muddy state.

'Oh, but he is very dirty, that one!' shrilled the boys delightedly, and Greer tried to explain between Pequeno's snorting, trumpeting and rolling that it was not the elephant but the creek bottom that had changed the water from sparkling diamonds to murky mud.

They went up the hill again, the mahout and two boys on Pequeno's back, Vasco and Greer following the big, carefully-placed feet to the strip of lawn by the house.

'Tonight,' directed Vasco before Greer went in to tidy up for dinner, 'we will leave the others to do what they wish while we have an early evening, for the ruined village is a longish run from Stuyva and we must be away by sunrise. Do you think you can be up at dawn?'

'I'm sure I can,' Greer promised.

She was. She was lacing up her brown plimsolls when he knocked on the door, and tying the knots she took up her cardigan and scarf and came out ready to go.

He looked at her briefly but approvingly. She wore slim fawn denim trews, a fawn shirt, and the jacket and head-scarf were brown.

'You are a boy,' he smiled, 'and a very sensible one. Also, as it will be dusty until we reach the hills the dust will not be obvious in that hue. Again, the wrap may be needed. The plain before we climb to descend again can be quite cool. Remember we have more latitudes than Bombay.'

He seemed pleased with her choice, and Greer got into the car. Vasco got behind the wheel and they skimmed down into the road from the village. For a while the route was familiar, she and Holly had used it on their explorations, then Vasco veered sharply north-west into a terrain that Greer had not yet experienced.

After a while they traversed some tea estates, well enclosed to keep out stray cattle and buffaloes. The plants, Greer noted, were laid out in mathematical accuracy, no haphazard rows here. It was not cropping time, so she missed the beauty of sari-clad pickers with bamboo baskets slung to their backs, but the planting itself was quite delightful, the close crops forming a large green umbrella through which no brown earth showed.

Soon the estates were left behind and they began climbing hills with shoulders of rhododendron and juniper, and a field flower that looked like a buttercup yellowing the track verge.

They stopped at the top to look around them, and for Vasco to indicate the course of that freak flood that fateful day, then they began to descend again. It did not take long to reach the bottom of the valley, and it did not take long for Greer to look around. For there was, as Mr. Gupta had said, as the Senhor had, simply nothing there. The flood had taken everything. Not a single reminder remained, and perhaps, Greer thought sadly, that was best.

She wandered along the empty valley, shivering a little when she pictured that awful day, though the Senhor had told her it had all happened in a flash, one moment there was a little village and people, the next there was no village . . . and only two small boys.

—Or three?

No, it was no use, Greer accepted at length, there was simply nothing to be gained here in spite of the fact that she had felt compelled to come. She turned back to where the Senhor waited by the car watching her. She started to go back to him. Seeing her turn, he called for her to wait where she was, that he would come to her. He got in the car again.

What happened then Greer could not have said very clearly. She heard the engine start, the car moved forward, then almost at once there was a dull bump. She saw that a large stone had come dislodged under one of the wheels and had lurched the car forward, and in the lurch Vasco had veered sharply forward and knocked his head. Fortunately for the control of the car another small boulder stopped any uncontrollable progress, but as it rocked to a standstill the unconscious man slipped from the seat to the floor. He was entangled there when Greer, breathless from running up the valley, opened the door.

'Vasco!'

He did not answer.

She knelt down and took his hand to find the pulse. It

seemed reasonable enough, so perhaps he had simply been knocked out.

She took a cushion from the back seat and slipped it under his head. She untangled the long legs and stretched them half out of the door. She found a little stream and soaked her handkerchief, came back and laid the wrung-out cloth over the forehead. When he did not come round fairly soon she began to worry. It must be more than a knock-out, it must be concussion. She knew that concussion needed warmth, so she piled up every cover and jacket she could find.

She took the pulse again, found it still satisfactory as far as she could judge, so decided to go for help. Help was not as unreasonable as it sounded; she had noticed a small village to the left of the hill as they had come down.

She hated to leave him, though; the heartbeat seemed normal enough, but should he come suddenly out of the concussion he might be confused and wander off. She stood a moment wondering what to do.

'Memsahib!' If ever a voice came from heaven, Greer thought, this little voice did. She turned thankfully to greet the speaker, to ask him to help her by going up to the village and telling them there what had happened. But, the urgent words on her lips, for a moment Greer paused. The little barefoot boy who looked back at her took the words away from her. Instead she simply stared.

'Memsahib!' He spoke again, and Greer recovered herself. She explained to him that there had been an accident, but saw that he did not fully understand. She supposed that in such an isolated village there would be little English spoken; it was different in Stuyva. But he was an intelligent little fellow, and he followed her gestures. With a nod of his dark head, he was gone.

Alone again, she checked Vasco's pulse, renewed the wet handkerchief. – But still wonderingly. *Wonderingly.* Why had she had that odd impact with that small boy?

Help came sooner than she expected it, and though the

English was disjointed she could follow it, make herself understood.

Vasco was carried up the hill, Greer following. She eventually followed the small procession into a small house. She checked Vasco's pulse again. A responsible-looking Indian also checked, then nodded an encouraging head. 'Time, memsahib,' he promised, 'time.'

'You are a doctor?'

'No, but one can tell. Just time.'

Greer thought rather on the same lines herself. She did not think that the Senhor was gravely injured, but she did think there was a concussion. She pushed a strand of the black hair from the olive brow and asked about doctors.

'None here, memsahib,' the Indian said. 'But time, as I told you. He will open his eyes and you can drive him back yourself.'

'You think that?'

'Oh, yes. The white of the eyes, the skin colour.' The man made a gesture with his hands. 'I think,' he said with that flash of teeth so typical of the Indian, 'that memsahib should rest.'

Greer felt a little tug at her side and saw the small boy again. He nodded for her to come with him. The Indian bowed a reassurance and seated himself patiently and protectively by Vasco's side. Aware all at once of a parching thirst, for evidently the episode had dehydrated her, Greer followed the child.

The clusters of simple houses seemed all the same to Greer, but the boy went to one on the right. Here, an Indian woman, who Greer supposed was the boy's mother, led her to a chair and put down a cup of tea. Oh, that Indian tea, Greer thought gratefully, enjoying the dark robust brew, smiling her thanks.

The woman, like the man, had a little English, and the two of them managed to talk. The sahib would be all right the woman encouraged, soon the memsahib could take him home, or if not to— She said the name of a village where there was a doctor, or so she had heard. She poured more tea.

Greer looked around the house. It was clean but small.

'Yes, small,' nodded the woman, 'for so many children.' She put up her fingers to tell how many.

'Boys? Girls?' asked Greer, and was told.

'But that one' . . . the woman nodded to the child who still lingered . . . 'not.'

'Not? Not your child?'

'No.'

'Which house, then?' For some inexplicable reason Greer knew she had to know.

'This house. My husband's aunt had him, but she died, so now . . .' A shrug.

'You mean he was her son? The son of your husband's aunt?'

'Oh, no, she was not young woman, that aunt. He good boy, but—' The woman tried to find a word that evidently eluded her, but was unsuccessful. 'He does not always want to play,' she said at last, and replenished Greer's tea.

But before Greer had time to drink it someone came to tell the memsahib that the sahib was recovered and sitting up.

He even could smile ruefully at Greer when she went into the room, apologize for causing her an inconvenience.

'Oh, Vasco, so long as you're all right,' she protested. 'Anyway, it was I, remember, who wanted to come.'

'And now you want to go home.'

'No, not entirely.' She was thinking suddenly and oddly of the boy. For some strange reason she felt curious about him. She did not speak to the Senhor of it, though. She only said what the Indian had told her, that there was no doctor here.

'But there is another village,' she began, 'where there could be medical aid.'

'Home,' Vasco Martinez chose. 'I'm feeling fairly fit again. I think I can even drive.'

'You're not driving, though,' she said severely, and she was glad that he did not argue. For Senhor Martinez to agree to a woman driving him, she thought, he must not feel as fit as he says.

She insisted that they wait until he drank tea. 'With sugar,' she stipulated, 'much sugar.' She explained, 'For shock.'

He allowed her to direct the number of lumps, and though he grimaced as he sipped the dark syrupy liquid, he drank it down.

After that Greer went down to the car and brought it up to the top of the hill to which the villagers had brought Vasco. Vasco got in, and Greer moved off.

The last thing to do with the little episode that she was aware of was the deep dark gaze of the little boy who had found them in the valley. He stood looking at them and not speaking, and again Greer paused. She had not even learned his name. All she knew about him was what his foster-mother had said.

'He does not always want to play.'

He does not always want to play. Again and again Greer turned this over in her mind as she curved down the hill, spanned the plain, passed the tea estates again.

'Vasco,' she said at last, unable to keep the little boy to herself any more.

But there was no answer, and when she turned to look at him Greer saw that the Senhor had lapsed into unconsciousness again. The boy now completely forgotten, she dug her foot down on the accelerator and the car fairly ate up the remaining miles.

CHAPTER NINE

'THERE is nothing broken, nothing sprained or strained. There is a concussion which is under control. Vasco is most certainly not in any danger, but on the other hand he is in need of some specialling.' Doctor Holliday took off his stethoscope and laid it down on the bedside table. In the bed, his eyes closed, everything about him immobile, was Senhor Martínez. On the other side of the bed Greer waited anxiously.

They had been nightmare miles ... the small boys would have corrected 'daymare' ... those last miles back to the Stuyva bungalow. Praying frantically that the usual livestock would be absent today, that no fig-seeking monkeys would impede her progress, no buffalo moving in slow and deliberate precision, certainly no goatherd with his goats, Greer had taken bends as sharply as safety permitted. As soon as the car reached the end of the drive, she had leapt from it, calling for help.

Fortunately the doctor had been sitting on the patio with Holly ... sitting very close to her, holding her hand in his ... even in her concern Greer had noticed that ... so within seconds he had taken over. Vasco had been carried to his room.

'For the first twenty-four hours after a knock like Greer informs us Vasco has suffered,' said Doctor Terry to the two girls, for both had followed the patient, 'the one concerned has to be closely watched.' He looked directly at Holly and nodded, and Greer felt the first resentment she had ever known against her stepsister stirring within her. 'There is a small but definite risk,' Doctor Terry went on, 'in any case of concussion that the victim will become unconscious again, due to haemorrhage on the surface of the brain. Mostly there are no complications, thank goodness, but one can still evaluate. You sit and watch him,

Holly. This is what you must look for.' Neither of them, Holly nor Terry ... and certainly not the inert Vasco ... noticed as Greer quietly left the room.

But even in the passage she could still hear Terry issuing his orders. Why? *Why?* Why was Holly being directed like this? Was it because when it came to Senhor Martinez it seemed a natural thing to couple her stepsister with him? But if this was so, why had Holly sat on the patio with her hand in the hand of the doctor? Why had she spent so many hours with Jim Matson, even confessed happily to a 'secret' she could not yet reveal?

It all made no sense to Greer. It also made for a pain she could not have credited, and, proudly, certainly did not intend to permit. Holding up her head, and it was difficult, for the events of the day had given her a throbbing migraine, she went to her room. She refused tea when it was brought to her, thinking wryly that had it been brought on the Senhor's orders the Senhor himself would have been on her threshhold at once demanding that she partake. Seeing that she did. But he was lying in his bed, still unconscious for all she knew, and Holly was watching him.

A second tap on the door, and Greer's choked, and the choke angered her, 'No, I told you before, I don't want anything,' was followed by a further tap and Doctor Terry's voice.

'It's me, Greer.'

'Yes?' She was on her feet at once, anxiety cracking her voice now instead of the choke thickening it. 'Yes? Is it Vasco?'

'Still not with us. Though I'm not concerned, at least not overly concerned. But I would be obliged if you would give our nurse a break.'

'Nurse? But I thought that Holly—'

'Nurse Holly,' he said easily. He smiled. 'Do you think you can take over while she snatches a rest?'

'Of course. Make Holly go to bed. She can't stand all this. I'll sit overnight.' Greer hoped Terry did not hear the eager note she could not keep out of her voice.

'No,' said Terry easily but firmly, 'just an hour or so would do. Holly particularly wants the night shift, and I think so, too.'

'You think so—' Greer looked at him blankly. She wanted to say, 'But you fool, Terry, if you care about Holly, and that scene on the verandah as I came back this evening certainly looked as though you cared, surely you wouldn't direct such a thing.'

But he had directed it, and a doctor's directions were orders, orders to be complied with, whether you agreed with them, or not.

'Very well,' said Greer, and followed Terry to Vasco's room.

Holly got up as they entered, smiled at Greer, said something that sounded professional to Terry, to which, surprisingly, or surprisingly, anyway, to Greer, the doctor nodded with all seriousness, then Holly went out.

Greer was still puzzling over it half an hour later, and getting no nearer a solution, when she noticed that Vasco was slowly ... very slowly ... surfacing again. She would have liked to have managed herself, but her good sense prompted her to alert the doctor, and he came in at once ... *bringing Holly*.

'Recovery will probably be ushered in by a vomiting attack,' he said briskly, and Holly nodded calmly, then took over.

Out in the passage again, Greer was aware that her fingernails were biting into her palms. She felt a hot prick of tears, a dryness in her mouth.

This time she did not walk proudly, she ran to her room.

She was not called upon that night, though hadn't the doctor said this? He had said, 'Holly wants the night shift, and I think so, too.'

The sensible thing would have been to accept it, have rested as much as she could so as to be fresh when she was needed, but Greer and common sense all at once were worlds apart. She, the responsible member of the family, the watch-girl, no longer weighed up pros and cons, made rational decisions, instead she lay wide-eyed throughout the entire night, letting processions of disturbing thoughts pass through her mind, with the result that when Terry tapped on the door the next morning to ask her to relieve Holly, by appearances Greer knew that *she* looked the night shift nurse, not her stepsister.

Indeed, Holly looked radiant. In all her life Greer had never seen her more radiant. Sitting by the sick bedside, Greer was relieved that the Senhor, now completely out of his concussion, the doctor had told her, at least slept. Those sharp dark eyes even in the less than alertness following the injury would have noticed her own shadowed eyes, the white line around her mouth.

But after she had sat by him for a while a peace came to Greer. She looked down on the handsome, if arrogant, features, and accepted something that she knew she must never admit, but something, too, that for a stilly moment she could admit, just to herself.

She loved this man.

Soon afterwards he opened his eyes, saw her and smiled. Except that she knew now that such a smile was for someone else, Greer could not have put that smile down, as she did, to Vasco's waking confusion.

She sponged his brow, put a cushion at his back, and by that he must have recovered his full senses, for he said quite awarely, 'So it is Greer now who watches me.'

'Yes. The watch-woman, remember?'

'I do not care to do much remembering just now,' he grimaced.

'Your head aches?'

'I feel it will if I try to think.'

'Then don't think. Would you like some tea?'

He said that he would, so she went out to get it, but when she came back, he dozed again, and the tea grew cold as she sat watching him.

It was Holly, back to take her turn, who had his full attention. Vasco was properly awake by then, and as Greer left she heard the patient and nurse ... Nurse Holly, as the doctor had said ... making happy exchanges as Holly propped him up to eat.

Feeling an abysmal failure, Greer sought out the little boys, who were taking lessons in one of the verandah alcoves. She sat behind them, ostensibly to 'observe', but really hearing nothing except those happy exchanges.

The children were doing some bookwork, their little dark heads were bent over the page. Not bent enthusiastically, that was apparent from the lukewarm flicking over when a leaf was done, the wistful glances outdoors. For some reason Greer found herself thinking of another little boy who was very different from these two. His mother ... *foster*-mother ... had said: 'He does not always want to play.'

Jim was absorbed, too, and though he flashed Greer a welcoming smile he did not stop what he was doing, and that was examine closely a written page. He read it several times, and it was only natural that Greer's glance dropped casually to the thing that so absorbed him. She could not see what was written, but she certainly knew Holly's writing as contrasted to the childish efforts of Chandra and Subhas. *Holly's* writing!

She sat on a while, but not 'observing' now, not even thinking in the strain that was required of her, thinking instead: What is this with Holly? *Who* is this? – Jim? Terry? ... Vasco?

She got restlessly up at last and went into the garden.

Gladly, by now, she would have stepped out of the watching of Vasco Martinez altogether, left it to others, so that when Terry found her some time later and said she would not be needed in the sick-room that afternoon as it had been decided to take Vasco into Senho, which was the nearest village with medical facilities for an X-ray, she was relieved.

Relieved, anyway, until Terry finished, 'Holly will

come with us.'

Greer nodded, not trusting herself to speak. But after they had gone, she lost her irrational resentment ... it must be irrational, she told herself, I must *make* it so ... in her concern for the Senhor. That concussion had lasted longer than it should. Had there been a damage? Was Vasco—

It seemed the longest afternoon she had ever put in. She took the children swimming. She took them walking. She filled in every minute with something, but still the time dragged.

Then at last the car was returning. Holly ... even more radiant if possible ... was calling, 'All's well,' and Terry was repeating the good news.

The Senhor was smiling at Greer, the same deep smile that she could have mistaken this morning had she not known better, so again Greer turned away, found something to do.

She could not be busy endlessly, though, and the Senhor remarked rather drily on this when he beckoned her over the next morning to sit beside him on the patio. Doctor Terry had advised several days of rest.

'So much coming and going,' he commented, 'such a busy bee. But all work and no play makes an unbright person. Right?'

'Dull,' she corrected.

'If it were not that you are the watch-woman and that a watch-woman must watch, I would say you are avoiding me.' He laughed ... but there was an inquiring note in the laughter.

She made herself laugh back. 'I'm here now, aren't I?'

'Yes, Senhorita Greer, you are here.' He tapped the tapered tips of his strong olive hands together for a minute or so, all the time directing his dark gaze at Greer. She tried to gaze carelessly back, but, to her annoyance, felt a flush rising, and turned her glance away.

'I wonder how the squirrel fared,' she said a little breathlessly.

'Do you, *senhorita*?' he asked deliberately. 'Are you wondering that?'

Another minute of fingertip tapping, then, 'You are not happy. What is it? I am quite well again.'

'You are imagining things, *senhor*. I am my usual self. And even if I wasn't, it wouldn't be because ... I mean ...'

'You mean it would not be because of me.' He smiled thinly. 'Very well then, you are happy.'

'I said my usual self,' she corrected.

'I do not believe your present state is your usual state,' he argued. 'I will concede that perhaps I should not have used happy, because I do not believe you have been *really* happy yet in your young life, cheerful, yes, bright, assuredly, but not deeply happy.' He took out his cheroots. 'I believe, Senhorita Greer, that *that* source in you has yet to be tapped.'

From the radiance in Holly *her* source of joy has been tapped, thought Greer, but she did not speak her thoughts.

He must have sensed that she was thinking of her sister, though, for he said, 'That *pequena*, that little one, has told you?'

'Holly?'

'Yes.'

'Told me what?'

'Then you do not know,' he smiled. 'Well, undoubtedly it is her privilege to keep it all secret until she is ready to tell. But I did think you might guess.'

'Oh, I have guessed.' Greer hoped she succeeded in keeping a bitter note out of her voice. Yes, I have guessed, she thought, but I have not arrived at *which* of the three. The doctor. The tutor. Senhor Vasco Martinez.

'Of course,' he agreed blandly. 'Why otherwise would she have tended me so carefully in my indisposition?'

It was too much. Greer went to rise. Then she saw that the Senhor was quite unaware of saying anything that could wound, so she steeled herself and sat back again.

She was thankful that his next words were impersonal. He asked how she and Holly had found the Stuyva countryside, and from there they went on to crops, comparing them to Australia's crops, and next to Portugal's.

He spoke so fluently of his country that she remarked rather in surprise upon that fact.

'Why not?' he smiled. 'Here is only my second home.'

But he was part of India, so much so she had imagined he had only spent his boyhood days in Portugal, perhaps afterwards a vacation upon occasion.

'Oh, no.' Another smile. 'I always go back and forth. I have this exporting business that my father and his father and several fathers again had before. It is a very old firm.'

'But although Portuguese you would be born in India?'

'No,' he said, 'the children are always born in Portugal.' He did not look at her but at the end of his cheroot, but Greer *felt* he was looking at her. It was such a strong feeling she cast around a little desperately for a reason for that intense feeling. The reason came to her. Holly, of course. He was intimating that her sister also would be going back to Portugal one day.

He broke into her thoughts with a description of his home village that she should have welcomed for Holly, but the white pots of red geranium in the courtyard of his villa that he spoke about, the gentle pastures beyond the villa so different from this intense Indian soil, the cork forests, the groves of tangerine, tore instead at her heart.

'Senhorita Greer,' she heard him say, 'you *are* unhappy. No, I will not have it that this is usual, something is not right with you. Can you tell me, please?'

'Oh, no.' No, he was the last person she could tell. Realizing she must sound rude, she said hastily, 'I'm not unhappy; I'm sorry I gave you that impression.'

'Why did you not go to Bwali?' he asked unexpectedly, and Greer knew that this time she could not answer that it was because the lilies were not yet out.

While she cast around for something to say, he spared her yet another subterfuge.

'Always Yaqub used to take his cares to Bwali,' he mused. 'I think we must do that.'

'I am the one who is supposed to have the cares, *senhor*.'

'Then I will take you, for unless I do so it seems you will not go yourself.' He *was* looking at her now, his dark eyes probing, trying to extract.

She did not argue with him. She was aware of a sudden immense lightness in her. At last she was going to the Pool. Pool of the Pink Lilies. Going with the Senhor. She trembled with an almost unbearable sweetness.

'You heard me, Greer?' he said softly. She could not remember him calling her that before – Senhorita Greer, yes, but never just her name.

'Greer?' he repeated.

'Yes, I heard you, *senhor*.'

'Vasco, please.'

'Vasco.'

'And we are going?'

'Yes.'

He laid down the cheroot and again tapped the tapered fingertips together. 'The Pool of the Pink Lilies,' he said.

But they didn't go.

Doctor Terry stopped Greer in the passage the next morning.

'Vasco said something about taking you to the old shrine. Put him off, please, Greer.'

'He's not well enough?' she said quickly.

'Perfectly well, but— To be frank, a distasteful thing has cropped up. I'm keeping it from him for a while. You know what he is, or you should know by now, no half-measures for Vasco in anything, be it approval, disapproval, love, rage, the rest.'

I certainly don't know love, she felt like answering, but she stood waiting for Terry to go on.

'He would pack up at once, race down.'

'To where?'

'The Bombay house.'

'Has something happened there?'

'Thieves,' Terry said. 'At least that's the gardener's report.'

'What have they taken?'

'Nothing, he says, or if they have then very little. But of course, he would not know what Vasco considers valuable.'

'Then shouldn't Senhor Martinez be told?'

'Eventually, certainly. But the thing's done, isn't it?'

'Yes,' she agreed, 'but if you don't intend telling him why are you asking me to put him off tomorrow?'

'More news might come that leaves me no alternative than to break the theft to him at once. I'd just like him to be around.'

'Very well then,' she said, 'I'll tell him I can't go.'

She told him that night. She stood on the patio with the others, but when they turned back to fix a rubber of bridge in which the Senhor declined to join, she declined, too. He seemed pleased, she thought ... but the look of pleasure was wiped out in a minute.

'You said you wanted to go.'

'No, Senhor Martinez, I said I would.'

'Perhaps you did, but your voice spoke more than that; your eyes did.'

'I'm sorry if you saw something that wasn't there.'

'I could make an order of it. You are after all in my employ. I could make it a day's duty.'

'I still wouldn't go.'

'I could force you.' His face was almost white with anger. At once he added coldly, 'But I won't. Don't be concerned. It is not something to be forced on anyone. Not Bwali.' He paused a moment, then he bowed.

'Good evening, Senhorita Greer.' He left her standing at the rail.

He sat around the next day. Greer had thought he might take Holly to the shrine, the boys, make a community party of it. He did not.

Terry told her that no further news had come from the Bombay gardener, in which event, even though Vasco would be angry later, he would keep the theft from him for several more days.

'He received quite an impact when he bumped,' Terry said, 'I would have no hesitation in telling an ordinary man about the report, but Vasco is not an ordinary man, he would start unturning stones at once, whether fit or not. Sorry to have kept you from that Bwali visit, Greer, but I didn't know what the news would be. Perhaps you could go tomorrow.'

'No,' Greer said, 'we won't go tomorrow.'

As she said it she did not think that she would be miles away from Bwali tomorrow, that the retinue of cars would be speeding back to Bombay.

It was not any further communication from the gardener that did it, it was a small memo book.

The proprietor of the village coffee shop had driven from town to bow politely and put it in the sahib's hand. He should have put it in the memsahib's, for the memsahib had left it behind, but the young lady was only an employee of the Portuguese gentleman. All the village knew of the importance ... and riches ... of the Portuguese Senhor.

'It was left, sahib, in my humble shop. The young memsahib. That memsahib.' The man bowed at Greer.

Duly rewarded, he bowed again, and went off smilingly, congratulating himself that he had not called too loudly that day, run too hard, after the memsahib's car.

Greer said, 'Is that where it was? I didn't have any occasion to think about it until yesterday. I'm sorry that you have been put to expense, Senhor Martinez. You must allow me to repay you for that reward.'

'It is nothing.' The Senhor made a dismissive gesture with his slim olive hand. The quick movement spun the book over. It opened at a page and remained open.

It was tea-time. All the household were on the patio to partake of tea and at the same time watch the boys feed Pequeno.

The Senhor leaned politely forward to take up the book to return it to its owner . . . then he stiffened and left the book, opened, where it was.

Greer was still unconcerned. There was nothing secret in the book. Only addresses. Only notes and reminders.

Reminders . . . Suddenly she was remembering a reminder she had jotted down to write to Arlene to tell her the new domestic arrangements at the Bombay house. Later she had done just that, posting the letter afterwards at Stuyva.

The fact had not occurred to her before, but it did, and with a sickening impact, now.

'I did not intend to see what you had inscribed, *senhorita*,' the Senhor was saying in a cool hard voice, 'but now that I have—'

'Yes, *senhor*?' Her own voice shook.

'Now that I have, why are my arrangements so important to you that you must note them down in a book? And who is Arlene?'

He only spoke quietly, but the flint in his tone had alerted the others. All heads were turned to Greer and Vasco Martinez. There was a dead silence.

Greer had no explanation to make. She had nothing to answer. As the silence grew, and grew, and they all still looked at her, she managed to blurt jerkily: 'I believe the doctor has something to tell you, Senhor Martinez.'

'To do with what is written here?' the Portuguese asked sharply.

'It could be,' she said wretchedly, for it *would* be to do with it, of course, what else? Yet she, poor fool, had not thought of this.

She turned to go, to – to run, but Vasco's voice stopped

her. 'You will remain, *senhorita*. And Terry, you will tell me something that it appears now I have not been told.'

'I didn't want to alarm you unless it was warranted,' said the doctor, 'and the gardener has assured me—'

'What gardener?'

'Aselmo.'

'But he is my Bombay man.'

'Yes,' Terry said. 'You see, the Bombay place was broken into ... nothing seems to have been taken, otherwise I would have—'

His voice trailed off in the face of Vasco's cold rage. The doctor shrugged across at Greer as though to say 'I told you so.'

But it was a gesture that Greer did not answer. She simply stood shocked and bowed. Shocked at what she had helped bring about, for it must be through what she had written to Arlene that this deplorable thing had happened. Bowed by that icy look in the Senhor Martinez.

Within an hour the household was packed up and on the road back to Bombay.

From a distance the 'cross-roads' city of India wore a dusky blue bloom, but as the cars came nearer to the teeming Bombay metropolis the inevitable enamelled, almost brazen skies glittered down.

Once more Greer was keenly conscious of the rather higgledy-piggledy construction style of the buildings, but between their un-planning that glorious blue shout of shimmering harbour that instantly took away any discordant note.

She sniffed once more the spices, herbs, jasmine and mango petals, she heard the clangour and clamour of the markets, the call of 'Only look, no need to buy' from the merchants, the crooning 'Two annas for a bunch of lilies, memsahib' from the girls.

Now they were in the city itself, passing the imposing government buildings, the banks and office blocks, the squares of flats. She remembered Uncle Randall's flat.

Then they were climbing ... how well she recalled that first anxious climb, the doctor in another car with Holly, she and the Senhor following, her instinctive thought as she had glanced out of the window that Holly would like this flower-soft street.

At last the Senhor's Bombay house was rising up. More a palace really ... no, a *palacio*, for it belonged to a Portuguese.

She thought of her first impression of the place, its almost breathtaking grandeur, and but for the dull heaviness in her she could have been affected once again by the white columns with their hanging baskets of fern, the flagged terraces with their tubs of yellow roses, the lavish lattice work.

'*Senhorita.*' They had stopped at the bottom of the lordly steps, and Vasco Martinez was bowing her out.

He put the tips of his fingers impersonally under her elbow to guide her up, but when he stopped briefly to issue an order as to the luggage she took the opportunity to hurry ahead.

Holly was not far behind her, and Greer braced herself for the question her sister must ask, that inevitable: 'Did you tell your uncle's wife that we would be away?'

But she had underestimated Holly. The girl, coming into the bedroom almost at once, only put her arms around her. 'Darling, I know it will be all right.'

'Holly, I didn't—'

'Hush! I don't have to be told.'

Tears were rolling down Greer's cheeks, but, oddly, they were not tears of sympathy for herself but tears of relief for Holly. For Holly was being the comforter instead of the comforted, Holly was being the watch-girl now. Holly was leading instead of being led. For a moment her present cares lifted. Greer felt a joy instead.

'You're well, you're really well, Holly.' Greer brushed her tears away and smiled at her sister.

'Yes, I feel I'm standing on my own feet at last. Oh, it's a wonderful feeling, Greer. You'll never know the futility

I went through, the desperation. You were fine, you devoted yourself to me, but just to know that I myself can cope ...' Holly gave a little shiver of joy. 'I wonder if that's why I felt so anxious to come here to India, I wonder if in some subconscious way I knew I could get better here.'

'The good part to me,' said Greer thankfully, 'is that we can go on now, Holly. You have the strength. When old Doctor Jenner said "...Why not? ... Let her go ... May as well..." I thought—'

'I often thought it, too,' Holly smiled.

'But he was wrong. And were he here he would not say "... Let her go" because he thought it couldn't matter, with your radiance he'd really be keen for us to move on. And we will, Holly. We'll go overland to England. How would you like that? There is a cross-country tour that I'm sure we could afford.'

Holly was looking at her in amazement. 'But, Greer, I'm not moving out. I – I thought you might have sensed that by now. I know I did say it was secret, but—'

Greer could not look back at her. She also could not bring herself to cry: 'But I don't know, not really, I mean there's been three of them, hasn't there, and though I know it could only be one ... *that* one ... what of the others?'

She heard her own voice say dully, 'But *I* must go, *I* can't stop here.'

'You are stopping here.' The voice at the doorway held no two thoughts about that. Senhor Martinez remained where he was, he did not enter. He said, 'You will remain anyway until I have looked into this matter. I will see you in my office in half an hour.' He turned on his heel.

Greer did not stop with Holly. She turned as quickly and single-mindedly as the Portuguese had, and went out of the big house by the back door.

She had intended to hail a cab, but when she saw one of the smaller house cars pulled up and empty behind the others, saw that the keys were still there, she simply got in. What she had to do, or at least whom she had to see, would not take long.

But she should have had more sense than to think she could get to Uncle Randall's flat and back in the stipulated time. She thought this some twenty minutes later. When would she learn to expect the inevitable hold-ups in an Indian street? The pedlars, the bicycles, the crowding taxis, the ever-appearing cow.

But at last she arrived there and ran up the stairs. For a moment she believed it would be as privately as she had thought it would be, and that was that Arlene had flitted off.

Then to her surprise the door opened. But not on Arlene. Nor Uncle Randall.

Senhor Martinez stood there.

'You are very transparent, Senhorita Greer,' were his opening words. 'I knew at once you intended this. I did not even have to check the cars. However, I have more local knowledge than you, which enabled me to be here to greet you.' He gave an ironic bow.

'I was coming back,' she said inadequately, 'I just wanted to see—'

'If your aunt was here? No, she has gone.' He shrugged.

'Has she taken . . . taken whatever it was that was taken from your house? That is, if it was Arlene who did it.'

'I think you can be assured of that.' He was fixing one of his cheroots, taking his time over the clipping and trimming and lighting. He looked at her obliquely across the blue weave of smoke.

'Why can I be assured?' she demanded.

'A simple but telling answer. Because what was taken only referred to your uncle and aunt.'

'Money—' she stammered wretchedly.

'I am a business man,' he said scornfully, 'I would not leave money in my house.'

'Then—?'

'Papers that your uncle gave me as a guarantee, a

guarantee of something that at no time did he ever intend to make good.'

'You were holding them as evidence against him?'

'Why not?' He exhaled slowly. 'While I retained these at least he could not do the same to others.'

'I don't think,' Greer said chokily, 'that that was your real reason. Uncle Randall had only to go to some other place, somewhere he was unknown, just as he has been doing all his life, to begin it all over again. I think you were only holding them to – to hold me.'

'Hold you? Why should I do that?' He laughed with soft amusement.

'I didn't mean it like that,' she flashed. 'I meant to hold something over me.'

'Isn't it the same?' he reasoned. 'So for that object you believe I retained these papers.' Again the soft amusement. 'Oh, no, you are very wrong. If I wanted to hold you, *senhorita*, it would be more like this.'

He had put the cigar down and stepped forward, but it was still all so quick that it happened before Greer realized it.

One moment she was standing a few paces from him, the next his hands were round her waist, gripped hard as his dark olive face came nearer to hers. She saw the black eyes, amused no longer, but burning, burning with a deep fire, a fire she could not comprehend, because it was Holly for whom those fires burned.

'Holly . . .' She tried to say it, but his lips were on hers, cool at first, harbour-cool, then the coolness going and Indian heat instead.

Slowly he broke the kiss. He held up his head again from hers. He released her.

'That,' he said with the soft amusement again, 'is how I would do it, *senhorita*, not with papers in a safe.'

'You – you're hateful!'

'So long as I have pressed my point.'

She went unsteadily to the window and held hold of the sill for support.

175

'What are you going to do? About Randall and Arlene, of course.'

'But of course.' Again the bantering smile. 'Who else?'

She ignored that. She said, 'Do you think that Arlene was supporting my uncle all the time?'

'Yes. Not from any wifely affection but for her own gain. She is well known in Bombay. She has never been any good. I would say' ... again he took up his cheroot ... 'that she made a good match in your uncle.'

'He hadn't deserted her, then?'

'He merely had found it convenient to lie low for a while.'

'But why did he bring us across? Why did he pay for Holly and me?'

'I think if you ever go into it, *senhorita*, you will find that Randall Perry and Arlene Perry were planning something quite large. But they needed an innocent face, two innocent faces, for their own were not innocent, not even where they were unknown. So—' He spread his palms.

'But if that was so, if we were wanted, would Arlene have been so antagonistic to us when we first arrived?'

'The bubble had burst. Randall had got out, leaving her to hang on until he planned another move, and that annoyed her. He probably did not know what move it could be then, but the opening occurred.' He smiled thinly and remindingly at Greer, and she flinched. 'His wife's attitude,' he went on, 'is understandable in such a person as she is, she would tolerate no friends unless they were profitable friends, and until you so conveniently came to her rescue, she had no use for you. Naturally then she was not pleased initially to see you. But afterwards, what a different story. Tell me, Senhorita Greer, how much money did you give her?'

'It was mine,' hotly.

'How much?'

She told him miserably.

He was smiling with thin amusement again. 'And I aided and abetted that by directing my accountant to pay you in advance,' he said.

'I was a fool,' Greer admitted quietly. 'But he was my uncle, my mother's only brother. Arlene was his wife. You will never understand that, Senhor Martinez. You don't understand the word belonging.'

His face had darkened at her words. For a moment Greer thought he was going to cross the room and either shake her or—

'On the contrary,' he said coldly, 'I understand very well. Belonging, to the Portuguese, comes first of all. But the belonged must always be worth the belonging. That is where you made your mistake.'

'Yes,' she admitted. 'I also made a mistake telling Arlene that we would be away, that there would only be a casual caretaker at the house. When I did so I was thinking of nothing more than my letters, hers to me, I was thinking how they would attract attention if they were held in the Bombay house for our return, alternatively if they were forwarded to Stuyva. I had no other thought, Senhor Martinez, and you'll have to believe me.'

He shrugged carelessly. 'Of course I believe that. What else? Do you think I suspected that you informed your uncle's wife with the direct knowledge that she would then ...' He spread his hands significantly. 'Oh, no, you have been foolish, but not malicious I think, even though there was no difficulty in getting into the house, even though' ... a sharp inquiring look ... '*it was done quite ordinarily with a key.*'

'You mean there was no force?'

'No, simply the turn of a key.'

'But my key, the one I was given, is still with me. It's here in my handbag. My – bag.' Standing almost where she had stood the last time in the flat, memory came flooding back to Greer. Her handbag tossed down. Arlene taking her out to the small verandah. When she returned her odd feeling that her bag was not where she had put it

177

... that her things, although they were still there, were not quite the same. She supposed now in their absence that the maid, instructed by Arlene, had taken an impression of the key. It would be easy enough.

'I don't know. Oh, I don't know.' She began to cry.

He came across to her and for a moment she thought he was going to put his arms around her in comfort, not like before in derision ... and something else, she dared think? ... more in gentleness and in friendship. Almost she raised her face in anticipation.

But when he came he just stood there.

'There is nothing to be done here, *senhorita*, we will go back to the house.' He paused. 'We will leave this discussion, all discussions, until tomorrow. It has been an upsetting period; for myself with that stupid accident as well. So instead we will rest. Then when we feel refreshed and calmer we will continue from where we have paused.'

'I want to leave Bombay, *senhor*,' Greer said emptily. She added, her voice firm now, intentional, 'Holly must come, too.'

'I can answer that for both of you,' he said at once. 'Holly, as surely you must know by now, will *not* leave.' He looked at her questioningly, questioning her for even thinking her sister would go.

'She has said so,' Greer admitted, 'but she could change her mind.' She waited a moment, then she looked questioningly, but questioning for a different reason, back at him. 'You can answer for both of us, you just said?'

'That is right, *senhorita*.'

'Then what do you have for me?' She tried to say it challengingly, but it emerged differently from what she planned.

He said coolly: 'That is not under discussion ... yet. But the other is. That "Who leaves?" of yours.' A pause. 'The answer, *senhorita*: No one leaves.'

'No one?'

'No one,' he said again. 'We are postponing the dis-

178

cussion, but not closing it. Meanwhile, no one leaves. As Holly had no intention of leaving, anyway, that really means you. *You are not leaving Bombay.* Now if you are ready we will return in my car. My man can bring the smaller one.'

This time the fingers under her arm were not so light. They impelled her out of the flat to the waiting limousine.

In silence they returned to the Bombay house.

CHAPTER TEN

GREER saw nothing of Senhor Martinez the next day, and only glimpses of Holly. Doctor Terry was packing prior to leaving for England. 'From there, who knows?' he said to Greer.

'I thought you were assigned here,' Greer replied, 'or at least somewhere in Asia.' To herself she added, 'That **rules out Terry for Holly, for she never could have kept** London a secret, not Holly. London was always to Holly what the Pool of the Pink Lilies was to me. No, it's not Terry, so why then did they sit hand-in-hand?'

'No assignment, I've just been enjoying a break between jobs,' Terry told her. 'I've restless feet, Greer, or perhaps I should say a thirst for more and more information, and not the sort in medical books but in different countries, in different people.'

Jim Matson took his small class as usual, but afterwards hurried off to his other pupils. 'I only got leave of absence for the Stuyva jaunt,' he explained. 'However, I'll be signing off from Bombay quite soon, I'm going to try my luck and my English classes in Madras.'

That ruled out Jim. It ruled out two.

But hadn't she known this? Greer said to herself as she sought out the little boys. She was rather unsure whether she was still in the actual employ of Senhor Martinez, in other words whether she was still required to 'observe', but she liked children, and it was no punishment to join the pair in the pool, to walk with them in the garden.

Last night, tossing sleeplessly in bed, Greer had resolved to speak directly with Holly at last. To ask her everything that Holly, and everyone else, meaning Vasco, seemed to assume she already knew. It was not going to be easy. To hear Holly say: 'Yes, it is the Senhor, of course, but I thought you had guessed' would never be easy.

However, she had to hear it, and resolutely Greer had gone first thing to tap on Holly's door.

It was pre-breakfast, yet Holly was gone. Greer had hardly believed it. Even allowing for Holly's remarkable change in health it seemed impossible that she was out at this early hour.

She saw her briefly later, but not to speak to. The little nurse who had attended her in her illness had come to visit her. The two sat by the window so deeply absorbed that Greer could not interrupt them. Later, Holly had been with Doctor Terry. Later with Jim. But not with the Senhor, Greer noted, though of course *he* would be reserved for those velvet, strangely disturbing Indian nights. But still I have to see her, Greer thought. Ask her. Know. Greer was not aware she said that *know* aloud.

'Know about us?' asked Chandra, squirting fistfuls of water at Subhas. 'Which one of us is the grandson of that grandfather and grandmother, you mean?'

'You know too much,' scolded Greer lovingly, for she had become extremely fond of the pair.

'We really do know a lot,' Chandra boasted. 'Shall we tell her, Subhas?'

'No,' said the other boy, 'remember what we were told.'

'Told what?' asked Greer idly, her attention more on herself and her cares. Then, all at once, for no possible reason she could have given, could have put a finger on, she knew she must know what these funny little atoms were being secret about. But to find out with this cunning pair one had to be as cunning. 'Not that it matters,' she yawned elaborately, 'for I am going away very soon.'

As she had guessed that apparent lack of interest disappointed them. 'Wouldn't you like to know before you go?' They stood before her very importantly.

'No,' she shrugged, hoping her assumed boredom would urge them on.

Piqued at that reply, they said together, as they always did things together and how it had puzzled her: 'It is this,

Gr – eer, we are brothers.'

Greer still pretended disinterest and yawned again. 'How do you arrive at that?' she smiled.

'We pricked our fingers with a pin and we have the same blood,' they said.

'Silly little boys!' What a fool she was listening to their prattle, for a moment just now she had felt—

'Also because Brother Mahsia said so.'

Now Greer's ears pricked, not those little brown fingers. She had never heard of Brother Mahsia before. A figment of their imagination? She stopped herself in time from saying 'Who is Brother Mahsia?' and said instead 'How would he know?'

'He would!' indignantly. 'He had us for many months. He did not want us. So many mouths and too little food, he said.' They sighed . . . in unison, of course.

'But he was left with us,' picked up Subhas ... or Chandra? ... 'our parents were very poor with many others to look after and twins were too many. That's what we were – twins.'

'When the flood came down that valley,' said the first boy, all secrecy forgotten now, 'and there were two children who were not found, Brother Mahsia said to the important men who were looking: "Here they are, they wandered up to my mission." '

'A mission?'

'Yes. For children whose parents are poor and have others to look after.'

'Go on,' breathed Greer.

'Brother Mahsia told us not to say anything, then you will be looked after and loved, he said. Later you can tell, he said, for it is not good to live always in a lie.'

'Now is later,' Chandra announced, satisfied. Subhas nodded.

It was nothing but fiction. Greer kept telling herself this. But somewhere, she also told herself, there is a possible ring of authenticity. For one thing these children are not imaginative children, they could never dream up a tale like this. For another thing, I have always believed they must be brothers.

'Did you ever hear of the other two boys?' she asked idly. 'The ones in the valley where the flood came through?'

'One boy,' they said together.

'No, two.'

'No, one,' they persisted, 'because we used to watch them play down there from our high hill, and that time of the water there was only one to play, the other didn't come.'

'And he, that one, was lost in the flood.'

Chandra looked at Subhas and Subhas looked back at him.

'It was bad,' they said together, 'but not bad for him, for that boy, for his ayah had taken him away, she must have seen the flood coming and taken him, but Brother Mahsia did not know where she took him, so he said as there are so many mouths to feed you can both be that boy, because they think there were two, and it is better to feed two than one.'

'He did not mean bad,' defended Chandra.

'And later he said we must tell,' said Subhas.

'Now is later,' they agreed.

'But why . . . why didn't you tell the Senhor? Tell the grandfather? Tell—'

They had started to play again. They were after all only little boys. Were they lying? Were they very shrewd? Were they gifted story-tellers? Or had it all happened, or something even remotely like it happened? Even very remotely was enough for Greer. Her mind running in a dozen directions at once, she called Ayah to take over their supervision and hunted for the Senhor.

He was not there.

She tried the doctor and he was away.

Jim. Gone.

No use to try Holly.

She sat at the window in her room and thought . . . and

thought . . .

For all its fantastic properties, somewhere in this story there was an essence of truth. A mission *could* have stood on the top of an overlooking hill, for look at the number of small villages clinging to the shoulders of all those hills. Two small boys *could* have been in the habit of looking down, that is if two small boys had previously been left in a mission run by a Brother Mahsia. There *could* have been such a mission, there *could* have been such a brother . . . Could! If! Oh, it was quite impossible.

But one thing Greer did know for certain, for wasn't the evidence out there in the turquoise pool?

There were two boys.

And – a third?

'No, one,' they had corrected her. 'That time there was only one. His ayah took him away.'

Took him where? *Where?* Odd to think that that village, so close, so – so impossible, also had a small 'unbelonging' boy. And a boy who '. . . does not always want to play.'

It was all too much, Greer thought. She got up. She went down to the garages. All the cars were gone. She did not know if a train went near the village, she only knew that a road and then a track went there. It was not such a formidable distance from Bombay if you left out Stuyva and cut in instead from the motor road. She knew approximately where, for she had seen it on the Guptas' and the Senhor's maps. It was a longish way, yes, but not impossible. It could . . . and it would . . . be done.

She checked her money. Enough, she thought. She remembered that hiring garage she had seen at the bottom of the hill.

Throwing a few things into a little bag in case she was delayed and had to stay, Greer hurried out, not waiting even to leave a note.

As she had expected, the garage proprietor spoke and understood English. Yes, he would hire Memsahib a car. He told Greer the price, and she opened her purse and withdrew the notes.

It was all a little too quick for the Indian. He wanted to bargain over it. Failing that he wanted to talk about it, bow and smile over it. In her anxiety to be gone, Greer withdrew more notes and pressed them on him. He protested, but she insisted. . . even a little sharply.

In ten minutes she was on the road. There was no worry about the right route, once you left the city you took the northern track and that was unmistakable because it was the only one. Besides, she found herself remembering it quite clearly.

She drove as swiftly as safety permitted, and she was fairly lucky, there were few obstacles today. She stopped several times for tea, sipping abstractedly as she asked herself what she intended to do. See Yaqub's parents first? Tell them what she had returned for? No, that would entail going into Stuyva, which was a long way round; also it could build up a hope that could be dashed down. Best to keep her plans to herself until she knew.

At mid-afternoon she arrived at the nearest turn-off to the hill village, and within half an hour was back in that small town, nodding to the people, who remembered her at once, smiling back at them as they greeted her, but going directly to the cottage where the small boy had taken her for tea.

The same woman met her, and did not seem at all surprised when she asked at once about the child.

'You liked him, then? Perhaps you would like to take him,' she said eagerly.

'I don't know,' answered Greer cautiously.

'Oh, he is a good boy, please know that, but it is hard, so hard. He is not my boy, remember I told you, and our food is not enough. We are poor.'

'Whose boy, then?' Greer asked.

The woman looked away.

'*Whose?*' insisted Greer. 'If I take him I must know.'

'My husband's aunt brought him. I told you that, too. We never asked why she came with the boy.'

185

'When did she come?'

'When she grew sick. She said that she must find the one who should look after him now that she was ill, but she died before she could do that, so we had the boy.'

'Do you think he was her boy?'

'Oh, no, she was not young. But when she *was* young, my husband told me, she was married and had a baby, but it died. I think that was why she did not give the boy to where he should have gone. I think she loved him very much. Have you come to take him, memsahib? Are you the one to whom he should go?'

'No, I am not the one.'

'But you will still take him?'

'Where is he?' Greer asked.

'He walks across to the old shrine. You will find him sitting there. A good boy, but he does not always want to play. Books, that is that boy. And looking at things. Yes, he will be at the shrine.'

'Shrine? Would – would that be the Pool of the Pink Lilies?'

'It was, memsahib. Now . . .' The Indian woman spread her hands. She went to the door, nodding for Greer to follow, and she indicated a track. 'It meets up with the road,' she said.

Greer stood silent beside her. She had known all these hill places were close to each other, Mr. Gupta had demonstrated on a map, Vasco had shown her with pen and paper, but only the woman pointing out the little path *really* brought it close.

She answered huskily when the woman asked, 'Shall I call a child to take you?' a choked 'No.'

'No,' she repeated more distinctly, 'no, thank you.' She fumbled in her purse and took out all she could find. It occurred to her, but without any impact, that she would have no money should she require petrol to get back tonight, no money should she stay on.

She went across to the little track. It was not very worn. Indeed, from the sparse imprint she would say it

186

was only used by one pair of small feet. It was well defined, though, and presently, just as Vasco had drawn these close-knit hills and their winding ways, the path met a dusty, bumpy road for the final quarter mile.

Now that at last she was coming to it, coming to the Pool of the Pink Lilies, Greer felt a trembling in her she had never known before. Ever since she had read that book those many years ago she had thought of India not in the terms of the Taj Mahal, Madura, other lovely shrines, but what she had seen when she had turned that page that day. The carved gods, goddesses and peacocks would be ruins now, she knew that, but the Golden Stairs? the Temple? the Pool? the lilies?

She turned a corner. Stopped. Felt a sharp sweet pain.

For the weathered old shrine standing a little crookedly before her was mirrored in a pool, yet not mirrored fully, for it could only be glimpsed in the water between a thousand lily pads, and those pads also could scarcely be seen, for the lilies, great, plate-wide, rose-pink lilies, were out. Their bloom covered everything, save here and there a water-mirrored corner of tower, cupola, aged gold stairs.

She stood enchanted. She stood breathlessly satisfied. She had always yearned to see this, and now . . .

'The memsahib likes?' She heard the little voice before she saw the little boy. He was sitting on a tuft of grass and staring, too, up at the old shrine, but he turned for a while to look eagerly at Greer.

'Oh, yes,' she whispered. 'Do you?'

'I like it very much.'

'And do you know why?' she came across to ask him. 'Do you remember?' No, of course he wouldn't remember; he was even younger, she could see now, than their own pair.

'I like it,' he said without any hesitation, 'because of all the things it wears.'

The things it wears. She looked at him incredulously. Then she said:

The raiment Bwali wears are these...
Saris of hills with folds of trees—'

She went on to the end, and he listened to every word.
He did not understand, not fully, but he smiled and told
her, 'I like that, memsahib.'

'Then you and I both like it,' she smiled back.

'And,' included Yaqub's son, for he was his son, Greer
felt sure of it, 'the sahib likes it, too?'

'Sahib?'

The little boy got up and salaamed politely to the other
side of the pink pond.

Senhor Vasco Martinez stood there.

Afterwards Greer could not have said how one moment
she was on one side of the Pool and the next moment,
with the child, standing with the Senhor.

But later Vasco said that he had run, too.

'We met,' he told her.

He told her then how he was not here this time because
he had read her mind, guessed what she was going to do.
No, he was not that much in tune. Not yet.

... Not yet?

'He was my garageman, that man from whom you
hired the car. You did an unwise thing when you over-
paid him, he knew you belonged to my household, and
because of that it was very important not to accept over-
payment. He came up to the house at once and told me,
for I had arrived home soon afterwards, how you had
hired the car.'

'He wouldn't know where I was going.'

'No, but the small tongues having been loosened refused to stop babbling. The boys sought me out and told
me what they had told you.'

'So you followed?'

'No, I took a much shorter track. Not only can I find
short ways in Bombay, Senhorita Greer, I can find shorter
country tracks, too.'

'But why would you come here? The Pool of the Pink

Lilies was never mentioned.'

'No,' he agreed, 'but I knew you must come.'

'Because of the boy?'

Vasco made a little gesture. He was looking deeply at her. 'You *had* to come – as I *had* to come. Because' . . . a pause . . . 'we were to meet here.'

And slowly, inevitably, with infinite tenderness, he took her in his arms.

She could have stopped there for ever, but it wasn't right, it mustn't be right – with Holly.

'Yes? Yes, Greer?' he asked. 'Your sister Holly?'

'You love her.'

'Very much. She will be my sister, too.'

'But you love her. *Love* her, Vasco.'

'Love her?' He looked a long moment at Greer. 'Oh, no.'

'No?'

'No.'

'Then – then Terry does?'

'No.'

'Jim?'

'No.'

'But—'

'You do not know,' he said. 'I see you know nothing, Senhorita Greer, nothing at all. Often I wondered . . . often I pondered over that . . .'

'Holly and Jim,' came in Greer stubbornly, eliminating the teacher first, 'spent long hours together.'

'Yes. Holly informed me she had to catch up so as to pass that exam.'

'Exam?'

'What else?' he smiled at her.

'The doctor,' said Greer next, 'he held her hand.'

'He was checking her pulse. He did it regularly. More than regularly when she had declared what she wished to be, for it was essential that she pass the health test.'

'Vasco – Vasco, what *is* this?'

He looked down on her. 'No,' he confirmed again, 'indeed you do not know. Then I will tell you, *pequena*, though it is a bore, for I have so many other ... tender ... things to do.'

'Tell me, please,' she insisted. She would not, must not, think of that 'tender' she *thought* he had said.

He did.

'Your little sister has never been as delicate as you feared. Not robust perhaps, but definitely not so needful as you and your old family doctor believed always to be handled with care.

'Terry recognized the case at once. You see although I spoke of three of us in England, Yaqub, Terry, myself, there was a fourth – Yvonne. She was frail, too. Or so we thought.'

'I believe,' put in Greer, remembering the doctor on her first night in Bombay, 'that Terry especially thought.'

'Oh, yes, he liked Yvonne. He liked her very much. But he treated her like a flower. Then another man came and treated her like a woman, and ...' Vasco shrugged.

'Poor Terry,' Greer said.

'Yes, poor Terry. But it was only beginning, and there will be others. Even someone we both know?' A little smile. 'Oh, no, I do not think that it was the end for him. Not like it would be with—' He stopped and looked soberly at her, and she yearned for him to go on.

But when he did it was on Terry again, and how the doctor had found in Holly a yardstick to Yvonne.

'So he knew how to work on her,' the Portuguese said.

'She had lessons from Jim,' Greer said next.

'Yes. I do not think that your sister had formal schooling as you did, Greer.'

'No.'

'Then she had much to catch up.'

'But – but for what?'

'For the entrance exam that hospitals demand. Maybe a hospital back in Australia. Maybe in England. Perhaps since our own nurse is seeing a lot of Holly, Holly will even begin her training here.'

'Training? Hospital training? Holly interested in nursing?'

'Yes, Greer. Surely you saw her delight in tending me when I was ill.'

'I – I thought her delight was in you,' murmured Greer.

'Did you? Did you, my love?' the Senhor said softly.

My love. *My love*. It couldn't be true. She wanted to take the words and imprison them in case she never heard them again.

... And then she was hearing other words, sweet, wild, abandoned words, so it didn't matter any more. Nothing mattered, nothing. Nothing with Vasco's lips on hers.

'I knew the moment I saw you that this was why my father's father's father had come to India,' Vasco was saying, 'I knew why I had seen this shrine as a boy and had known that one lovely, lovely day ... Oh, Greer, little watch-girl, I think I have been watching for you ever since then – no, longer than that, I have been waiting for you from the day I was born.'

'I didn't know Portuguese were poetic.' She said it indistinctly, for it was hard to talk pressed so close to him. 'I thought that was for Indians. Pale hands. Yellow roses. And then the poetry of Yaqub.'

'And Yaqub's son?' he asked.

'Vasco, we don't know that yet.'

'I think we will. But before I try, my Greer, will you mind giving him to his grandparents?'

'If they are,' she said.

'But will you mind?'

'No, he would belong there.'

'And what of two small imps who belong nowhere, who were left because their parents had so many others, too many, so Chandra—'

'Or was it Subhas?'

'One or the other,' Vasco smiled, 'said. But what of

191

them, Greer? Back to the mission again?'

She was looking aghast at him, saying, 'Surely you are not asking me that.'

'But I am. Two children before we even begin!'

She loved that. She tasted it and loved it. She saw a little boy with Vasco's eyes, a little girl with Vasco's hair, a—

'You have not answered,' he said.

'It could make no difference. I love our two.' Then she remembered the little boy, sitting on a rock now and staring at the Pool of the Pink Lilies, and added, 'Our three, perhaps?'

'Perhaps,' he smiled. 'With the six or seven we plan what is one, two or three more? But first let us see, Greer.'

She watched him look to the child, she heard his voice call softly, 'Ayub ... Ayub!' for that had been the name that Yaqub and Lalil had given their son.

At first nothing happened. Then the boy stirred. He turned. The smallest of frowns creased his little forehead as unconsciously he heard a mother's gentle beckoning, a father speaking to him. He listened a moment, then turned back again.

'He is,' marvelled Greer, 'oh, Vasco, he *is*!'

'Yes, indeed, he is. Are you sorry, *pequena*?'

'For myself, yes, for the Guptas glad.'

'And for us?'

'With six, you said? With seven?'

They smiled at that ... and Ayub, looking across at them, remembered in a kind of dream other smiling, and smiled, too.

Part of the smile smiled back from the Pool of the Pink Lilies.

Let Your Imagination Fly Sweepstakes

Rules and Regulations:

NO PURCHASE NECESSARY

1. Enter the Let Your Imagination Fly Sweepstakes 1, 2 or 3 as often as you wish. Mail each entry form separately bearing sufficient postage. Specify the sweepstake you wish to enter on the outside of the envelope. Mail a completed entry form or, your name, address, and telephone number printed on a plain 3"x 5" piece of paper to:
HARLEQUIN LET YOUR IMAGINATION FLY SWEEPSTAKES,
P.O. BOX 1280, MEDFORD, N.Y. 11763 U.S.A.

2. Each completed entry form must be accompanied by 1 Let Your Imagination Fly proof-of-purchase seal from the back inside cover of specially marked Let Your Imagination Fly Harlequin books (or the words "Let Your Imagination Fly" printed on a plain 3" x 5" piece of paper). Specify by number the Sweepstakes you are entering on the outside of the envelope.

3. The prize structure for each sweepstake is as follows:

Sweepstake 1 – North America

Grand Prize winner's choice: a one-week trip for two to either Bermuda; Montreal, Canada; or San Francisco. 3 Grand Prizes will be awarded (min. approx. retail value $1,375. U.S., based on Chicago departure) and 4,000 First Prizes: scarves by nik nik, worth $14. U.S. each. All prizes will be awarded

Sweepstake 2 – Caribbean

Grand Prize winner's choice: a one-week trip for two to either Nassau, Bahamas; San Juan, Puerto Rico; or St. Thomas, Virgin Islands. 3 Grand Prizes will be awarded. (Min. approx. retail value $1,650. U.S., based on Chicago departure) and 4,000 First Prizes: simulated diamond pendants by Kenneth Jay Lane, worth $15. U.S. each. All prizes will be awarded.

Sweepstake 3 – Europe

Grand Prize winner's choice: a one-week trip for two to either London, England; Frankfurt, Germany; Paris, France; or Rome, Italy. 3 Grand Prizes will be awarded. (Min. approx. retail value $2,800. U.S., based on Chicago departure) and 4,000 First Prizes: 1/2 oz. bottles of perfume, BLAZER by Anne Klein. (Retail value over $30. U.S.). All prizes will be awarded.

Grand trip prizes will include coach round-trip airfare for two persons from the nearest commercial airport serviced by Delta Air Lines to the city as designated in the prize, double occupancy accommodation at a first-class or medium hotel, depending on vacation, and $500. U.S. spending money. Departure taxes, visas, passports, ground transportation to and from airports will be the responsibility of the winners.

4. To be eligible, Sweepstakes entries must be received as follows:
Sweepstake 1 Entries received by February 28, 1981
Sweepstake 2 Entries received by April 30, 1981
Sweepstake 3 Entries received by June 30, 1981
Make sure you enter each Sweepstake separately since entries will not be carried forward from one Sweepstake to the next.

The odds of winning will be determined by the number of entries received in each of the three sweepstakes. Canadian residents, in order to win any prize, will be required to first correctly answer a time-limited skill-testing question, to be posed by telephone, at a mutually convenient time.

5. Random selections to determine Sweepstakes 1, 2 or 3 winners will be conducted by Lee Krost Associates, an independent judging organization whose decisions are final. Only one prize per family, per sweepstake. Prizes are non-transferable and non-refundable and no substitutions will be allowed. Winners will be responsible for any applicable federal, state and local taxes. Trips must be taken during normal tour periods before June 30, 1982. Reservations will be on a space-available basis. Airline tickets are non-transferable, non-refundable and non-redeemable for cash.

6. The Let Your Imagination Fly Sweepstakes is open to all residents of the United States of America and Canada, (excluding the Province of Quebec) except employees and their immediate families of Harlequin Enterprises Ltd., its advertising agencies, Marketing & Promotion Group Canada Ltd. and Lee Krost Associates, Inc., the independent judging company. Winners may be required to furnish proof of eligibility. Void wherever prohibited or restricted by law. All federal, state, provincial and local laws apply.

7. For a list of trip winners, send a stamped, self-addressed envelope to:
Harlequin Trip Winners List, P.O. Box 1401, MEDFORD, N.Y. 11763 U.S.A.
Winners lists will be available after the last sweepstake has been conducted and winners determined.
NO PURCHASE NECESSARY.

Let Your Imagination Fly Sweepstakes

OFFICIAL ENTRY FORM

Please enter me in Sweepstake No. _____

Please print:
Name _____

Address _____

Apt. No. _____   City _____

State/   Zip/Postal
Prov. _____   Code _____

Telephone No.   area code
( )

MAIL TO:
HARLEQUIN LET YOUR
IMAGINATION FLY SWEEPSTAKE No._____
P.O. BOX 1280,
MEDFORD, N.Y. 11763 U.S.A.
(Please specify by number, the Sweepstake you are entering.)